REIGN OF BLOOD

Rietta Boksha

For my father,
Who raised me with a warrior's heart and a poet's fire.
You taught me to stand tall in storms, to speak truth even when it trembles,
And to carry honor like a blade across my back.
This saga is for you—
For every story you never stopped me from telling,
For every battle you believed I could win,
And for the bloodline of strength you passed down like a shield.
May your name echo in every hall I walk.
May you know your legacy lives in mine.
Skål, Dad. This one is yours.

CHAPTER 1

I can't see.

Everything around me is black. Pain shoots through my right leg. When I reach down to find out why, it becomes immediately apparent. The bottom half of my leg is gone, leaving behind a rough, wet edge that makes my stomach swell. What is going on around me fades into view.

It is a mix of fiery warfare and... a bedroom. Am I dreaming? The pain is so real, but why would I be fighting? I try to scream for help, but no sounds come out—the battle around me just wages on. A snow-white sword lies at my side. The end is covered in deep crimson, but the rest remains eerily beautiful.

I feel pulled to it, like it belongs to me, but how can it? I run my fingertips along the long blade as it vibrates beneath my touch. Just as I reach the hilt, I'm blasted backward. My body flails, and when I finally dare to open my eyes, there he stands.

My brother, Espen.

"Another one of your vivid dreams, sis?"

"I would call it a nightmare but there's no point splitting hairs over it."

"What was it this time?" he asks, taking a seat on my bed. The weight of his body rolls mine closer.

"I was in a battle but losing."

"Why would you say you were losing?" He plays with the long leather braid of his necklace.

I push myself up to sitting, my upper half leaning into the headboard as I cross my now fully intact legs. "The bottom half of my leg was gone."

"Yeah, that isn't a good sign..."

"I did have this beautiful sword, though," I say, bringing the sword's vision back to the forefront of my mind.

"Well then! It sounds like it's time to train again."

I try to stop myself from rolling my eyes, but it is an impossible task. "You know Father doesn't like that, Espen." I turn over onto my side and attempt to move to the opposite side of the bed, but he grips my arm before I can get far enough away.

"He is not here, Brynja. You know I would never put you in danger. That's why I insist on training you. I won't always be around to protect you."

I know he is right—he usually is. My big brother has guided me since the day I was born, but his ego doesn't need to know that. I remain still with my back to him. His slow, steady breathing could lull me back to sleep.

"Come on, Brynja."

When he doesn't affectionately refer to me as sis, I know he is being serious.

"Fine."

"Meet me at our place in ten."

As soon as he is gone, I already miss his presence. My father has never been interested in me. As with most kings, he wanted a flock of heirs. I'm merely a "useless" princess. It's why he doesn't let me train. Women don't train. They tend to the men. Which is interesting, considering he married the strongest woman I have ever encountered.

My mother is a force on every level. She is firm, steadfast, and a committed powerhouse. I possess many of her qualities, but they have been muted by my surroundings and circumstances. Many believe I am lucky and that I should be thankful for what I have. If they only knew. I am a princess, but I am shackled. I'm smart enough to know when to push and when to bow my head.

I change into my solitary training outfit, one that Espen put together for me piece by piece. A rugged pair of brown trousers, brown boots, and a royal blue form-fitting tunic make up the base layer. Over that, I place a small section of chainmail that stops just above my ribcage. On top of that is my favorite part, the brown shieldmaiden armor complete with a pair of bracers. There is no way to wear this and not feel like a warrior.

A glance in the mirror reflects the same image—the image of who I want to be but am forced to keep in a cage. My long blonde hair trails past my waist, which I quickly divide into two and braid out of the way. I may be training with my brother, but he doesn't go easy on me—ever. I storm away from my reflection and head to meet my brother.

Just past the outskirts of the castle property is Vildmark, a wild piece of land left entirely untamed but still within the city of Thornheim. Not many venture here for fear of what they may stumble upon, which makes it the perfect place for Espen and me to train.

"I was starting to wonder if you were going to chicken out."

I refrain from taking the bait and instead hold out my hand for my sword. I tried to convince Espen to let me keep it in my room, but he refused to risk it. There would be no convincing way to explain why I had a sword in my room, so I resentfully agreed. The moment the hilt touches my palm, my body thrums with energy. I move slowly, slicing side to side as my body adjusts to the powerful extension.

"You move so naturally, Brynja, you need to learn to trust that."

"Are you saying that I don't trust it?"

"I'm saying you think too much."

Before I can respond, he charges me. I get my sword in position and our blades clang together. I press my weight into him and attempt to whirl around him when he drops to his knees and rolls between my legs. His blade finds my throat, and in mere seconds, I have been defeated.

"Don't give up. What now?" he asks as if he can read my thoughts.

"I... don't know."

"Yes, you do. Stop listening to your brain and listen to your body. How is it telling you to escape?"

We go over this every time, and I don't know another way to tell him that my body doesn't talk—only my mouth does.

"Get out of your damn head. Take me down! Now!"

The thrum of energy in my body increases, but so do my

thoughts as I race through every option I can think of. Most require me to shed some blood and none promises survival.

"She can't do it."

The energy in my body changes from fire to fury instantly. Anyone else could say it and I would brush it off, but his voice alone makes me want to spit venom.

"Agnarr, not now," my brother says, his sword pressing slightly harder into my throat at the unexpected appearance of his best friend.

"Why not? Battlefields are not a comfortable place. Training her in comfort teaches her nothing, Espen."

"That may be true, but we need to get a foothold first. Not just toss her to the wolves."

"I know a wolf. I'm sure he would be happy to earn an easy meal."

I can feel my brother's pulse quicken as he gets more and more agitated with Agnarr. He steps away from me and throws his sword. It lands well over fifty feet away, sticking straight into the ground.

"Alright, you train her." He crosses his arms, eyes locked on me.

I may not be good with a sword yet, but I know how to shoot daggers with my eyes. When I glance over at Agnarr, he gives Espen the exact look I am. Thank the gods. I have a hard enough time training with my brother. I can't imagine how frustrating training with Agnarr would be. I might kill him.

"What, you're just here to give me Hel but not actually be useful? If that is the case, be gone. I'll come find you for a drink later."

"Go get me your sword you tossed like a child, and I will teach *this* girl how to fight like a real warrior."

Hels. So much for slipping away.

"Ready yourself, Princess. I will not go easy on you," Agnarr says, his back to me. He doesn't even want to look me in the eyes, which gets me ruminating. Has he ever looked me in the eyes? Before I can finish my thought, he charges at me. This time, instead of waiting for his sword to meet mine, I lunge forward. Our swords collide with a heavy clang. His muscles flex against mine, and I have to stagger my footing just to have a chance at staying upright.

"It's not just about strength. Use your wits. If you have any." He takes another metaphorical stab at me.

He may be telling me to use my wits, but he is using all his strength. The longer I hold against him, the harder he pushes. I wait until he has me almost completely off balance before ducking to the side. The abrupt movement causes him to fall to the dirt. My brother roars with laughter.

"It seems she has more wit than you, Agnarr."

He is on his feet and charging me once again. I manage to get my sword in front of me but not in the proper position, and he sends me flying. I land flat on my back with him sitting on top of me. I struggle against his weight, but it is much harder to defend in this position. I reach for his arm, but the moment I touch him, it is like I have been struck with a thunderbolt. Electricity sizzles through me and a completely different world appears before my eyes.

Everything is white and glowing. I feel utterly weightless as air swoops around me in fast waves. There is a man with a white beard, but the rest of his face is hidden by a cloak. He has a sword as long as his body and a...

Just as quickly as the vision came, it's gone. I am back lying on the ground, gulping for air. Espen is on one side of me, Agnarr on the other. My brother's eyes are laced with fear and confusion. I reach up slowly to touch his face, and thankfully, nothing happens. Just my hand being greeted by his familiar scruffy jawline. My touch seems to calm him as much as it does me, so I move my attention to Agnarr. Our eyes meet for what I'm convinced is the first time. He has the darkest blue eyes I have ever seen, like the color of the sky just before sunrise.

Worry surrounds the edges of his eyes, and he is trying to cover it with annoyance. One trait I inherited from my mother is her ability to read people's emotions, but I have always struggled to read Agnarr. I could never figure out why, but the moment our skin touched it's like a gate was unlocked. He can no longer hide. I can't help but smile.

"What are you smiling for, Princess?" he asks, still trying to act like he is annoyed.

"I'm sorry, did I hurt you, Agnarr?" I reach for my brother's hand and he pulls me to my feet.

"Hurt *me*? You are the one who ended up on their backside, not me." He crosses his arms over his chest.

Wait? Did he not feel it too? Whatever *it* was.

"You didn't feel it?" I ask, looking back and forth between the two of them. They both look at me, perplexed.

"What are you talking about, Princess? I didn—

"Stop fucking calling me Princess, Agnarr."

Espen walks over and puts a hand on my shoulder. It's always been his subtle way to help calm me. I don't get angry very often, but when I do, it can be explosive.

"What did you feel, sis?"

I decide to ignore Agnarr entirely and turn my attention to Espen.

"It felt like I was struck by lightning, and then I... I saw something."

Agnarr laughs and lifts his arms, snarling in frustration, but not Espen. The fiery amber color of his irises swirls like a hurricane in the depths of the sea as he digests what I just said.

"How come this has never happened when you touch me? Or anyone in our family?"

He poses a logical question I don't have an answer to, but I also have a feeling that whatever happened wasn't rational either.

"I don't know. I'm just as shocked as you are. Literally." I rub my arm where I can still feel leftover tingles.

"You can't be serious? You don't think that was real, do you, Espen? That was merely a tactic to get me to take it easier on her."

Espen's eyes meet mine briefly before turning to Agnarr. "Of course, I believe my sister. She has never given me a reason to doubt her."

"She is a woman, that is all the reason you need."

"I feel sorrow for your sisters. Now come over here and let her touch you again."

"There are numerous things wrong with that sentence, but I'll pass. Let me know when you are ready to do—"

"Agnarr, Enough with the nonsense and just come here!"

I do not know much about my brother's best friend, but I do know he is not one to take orders. So, when he walks over to us and willingly holds out his arm, I am stunned. I slowly reach for him in an attempt to prepare myself for what will happen next. I wrap my hands around his powerful forearm and... nothing.

I try moving my hand to different locations on his arm, but nothing happens.

"See, it was all just for show. Can I go now?"

"Since you had no reason to be here in the first place, go. You have wasted enough valuable time."

Agnarr opens his mouth to say something else but changes his mind and storms off instead. He frequently shows up unannounced and I have never figured out why. Especially since he expresses such a distaste for me. I also can't help but wonder how he always figures out where we are. It is not as if we announce our plans to the world. Quite the opposite, actually. Most things between me and my brother are secret. The only other person who knows where I go and what I do is my servant, Thyra. She has been by my side since I turned twelve. Barely a teen herself but born into a family with no money means you do whatever is necessary to survive. Her father sent her to us and has not laid eyes on her since.

To me, she has never been a servant. She is a friend, a companion—the sister I wish I had been born with. But this, too, is a secret. It cuts me every time I'm forced to treat her coldly in my father's presence, but if I don't... he'll send her away. Or worse—kill her.

Espen spends another hour training me. Sweat coats my entire body and everything aches, but with each attack, I improve. My movement becomes more natural, and even though I feel weak with exhaustion, I also feel increasingly strong. Espen and I have trained many times over, but something is different today. Something has changed and it all goes back to my internal lightning strike. It not only unlocked the door to Agnarr's emotion but something deeper... in myself.

"Again!" I roar at Espen.

"Brynja, you have already proven yourself today. You are tired and Father will be home soon. It is time to rest."

"Again."

He pretends to walk away in an attempt to disarm me, but I know better, and instead of waiting for his surprise attack, I charge him. Before he can turn around, I am mere inches from him. He can't get his sword up in time and is forced to use his forearm to block me. The blade digs into his bracer, but the combination of aged leather and bone is enough to stop it from causing any real damage.

"What now, dear sister?" he asks, baring his teeth as he pushes back against me.

"Now I kill you."

In one swift movement, I side pivot around him and take his back side. For the first time in years, my sword finds his throat.

He remains still, the only movement coming from his chest laboring with exhaustion. My arms are heavy with their own exhaustion, but I refuse to release him. It has taken a long time to get here, and I plan to relish in it.

"You win, okay. Can you please release me before I collapse and kill myself on your sword?"

A grin radiates across my face. That is all I needed to hear. I release him and he promptly falls to the ground.

"You don't need to play dead, Espen. You saying I win is enough. Come on, let's get back."

"I need five minutes. Plus, we need to come up with where we were in case Father asks."

I lie down next to him. The sky is on the cusp of transitioning from day to night, causing a beautiful mix of colors. Deep orange, rosy pink, and inky plum mingle in front of my eyes. We rest in silence, our shoulders scarcely touching each other. This isn't the first time we have done this. I doubt it will be the last. Neither of us will say it out loud, but the slight touch of our shoulders brings more comfort than anyone can imagine. The last time we were like this, the only thing we were looking at were bricks and the floor was as cold as ice.

"Stop thinking about it," my brother says, reading where my thoughts are going again.

"I can't help it."

"Yes, you can. Just like you all of a sudden unlocked your warrior, you can lock away those... horrific memories."

"How do you do it, Espen? Just... forget like that."

"Because I only make room for what is important." His hand finds mine and gives it a gentle squeeze. "Now where were we?"

Thyra is waiting for me at the gate when we finally make it back.

"Come, I have a bath drawn. Let's get you cleaned up."

Espen and she make brief eye contact before he gives her a wink and runs off.

I strip off my clothes and attempt to hide them away when Thyra takes them from me. "Get in the bath while the water is still hot, Your Royal Highness."

"Thyra, you don't have to d—"

"Just go, Brynja. You never know who is listening. Let me handle this."

I may disagree but fighting with Thyra is not going to help anything, so I do as requested.

The hot water consumes me and brings instant relief to my aching muscles. I sink beneath the surface and enjoy the silence. That is one thing I don't have enough of in my life. Peace. Peace and...stillness. I hold my breath as long as I can under the water to enjoy what little peace I find. When I finally surface, Thyra immediately starts washing my hair.

"Seriously Thy—"

"Be quiet and let me wash your hair. This is a chore I enjoy doing," she says, putting air quotes around chore.

"Does that mean I get to wash your hair next?"

"In the next lifetime, ma'am." She goes back to being

formal instead of calling me Brynja. The fear she has of my father overhearing her "misbehaving" is real. It has only ever happened once, but the punishment lives within both of us. I remain quiet while she finishes tending to my foul-smelling body, and I listen to the racket of the palace.

I wonder what my life would be like if I lived anywhere but here…

The cool ocean breeze swirls around me, reminding me I haven't left the palace grounds in far too long. Yes, I trained with Espen yesterday, but our secret jaunt into the woods doesn't count. I miss the beach—the warmth of the sand between my toes… and the twins beside me. Espen and I have been friends with the twins for as long as I can remember. For just as long, my father has disliked our friendship, saying there is something "off" about them. I don't know how he can form such a strong opinion when he has only spent a total of a few hours with them over all the years.

"Why don't you go to the beach today?" My mother's warm voice spills over me as her hand finds my lower back.

"You know Father hates when I leave and even more so when it involves the twins."

"You let me handle your father."

I turn away from the balcony view to face her. Her soft features and one-of-a-kind smile immediately warm my soul. She is breathtakingly beautiful. Her long blonde hair cascades over her shoulders and her amethyst eyes portray both tenderness and strength.

"You are not a child anymore. You are a woman and he needs to treat you as such."

I can't stop myself from rolling my eyes. There was a

time when my father acted like a loving parent, but that changed when the war broke out. The only logical explanation we have come up with is the leader of the rebellion is Thoracian. My mother is also Thoracian, meaning my brother and I also have Thoracian blood running in our veins.

That never used to matter to him. He actually broke numerous royal laws just to marry my mother because he was so in love with her. Born in the beautiful meadows of Thora to a family of jewelry makers, she was far from royalty. My father was looking for a necklace for his mother for her birthday. The amethyst eyes and breathtaking presence of Anitra Thorsson captivated him. Now who she is disgusts him. All because of Sigvard.

I don't even blame the rebellion. My father rules with an unforgiving iron fist. Almost any crime committed is punished by slavery. If it's not slavery, it's death. This has only gotten worse with the rise of the rebellion. Now our world is controlled by fear and blood. There is no love. That is why my brother insists on training me. I was never drawn to the sword, to battle, but I can't deny the moment I started training, it ignited something deep within me. I thought it was just the desire to prove my father wrong. That I am far more than a princess, but after yesterday there clearly is something else.

"Go. Stop standing here with wandering thoughts and go be free."

As much as I love my mother's sentiments, I have to stop myself from laughing. Free? Free is nothing more than a word on the wings of a dream.

"Stop arguing with me in your head and go before I change my mind."

I offer her a quick curtsy and do as requested before my father appears.

When I arrive at the beach, it is empty. Nothing but the sound of crashing waves and the smell of sweet, salty air. Taking a deep breath, the cool air cleanses my soul. The scent may reach the castle, but it's true smell is tainted by the vile presence inside. I remove my shoes and step onto the sand. The warmth mixed with the grittiness of the sand is much like my life. There are moments of comfort but along with it comes much ache. I take several steps, letting it press between my toes before finding a spot to sit. Legs crossed and eyes closed, I dream of a different world.

A small house atop the rolling hills of Rosvin, a humble town not far from my mother's homeland of Thora. I fell in love with it one summer and swore to make it my home one day. My mother and brother living a field away. A man to tend to my every need. The thought has me aching. It has been far too long since I have been touched, but I force my focus back to my pretend world. A horse. All white to gallop through the fields so fast my hair never touches my neck.

"What do your dreams hold today, Bryn?" Astrid's voice brings me back to reality.

"The usual. A life of simple pleasures."

"Why go simple when you can create anything you wish?"

"Because you know just as well as I that having everything can be torturous, to say the least."

She sits behind me, pressing our backs together. A small surge of pain curls up my spine but is quickly replaced by the warmth of her presence.

"It has been far too long, my friend. Has your father tightened his grasp once again?"

"Is it ever truly loosened?"

"I would love to loosen other things." Aksel's husky voice floats over us.

I knew he would not be far. The twins are never apart, which has always left me curious about how they handle... intimate moments. As curious as I am, his bed is one I would never willingly enter. He may be devastatingly handsome, but there is something dark behind his eyes.

"That is my sister you speak of, Aksel." Of course, my brother could not leave me either.

"Just because she is your sister does not mean I am blind to her beauty. How many others have you seen with eyes like hers?"

My brother laughs and turns away. Arguing with Aksel is useless. He has tried for years to win my favor and only death will stop him.

"Her eyes are a blessing from the gods themselves," Astrid says, pushing more weight against me. For years, different tales have been spun about my eyes. My right one is the color of the iolite stone, but my left is half iolite, half brown. Split perfectly down the center like a lightning bolt striking a tree. Astrid is one to talk. She is beautiful. Her medium-length, wavy blonde hair perfectly cascades around her shoulders. Her skin is slightly sun-kissed, and her eyes are periwinkle.

"Maybe she is truly a goddess hiding among us lowly humans," Aksel teases, his voice still thick with flirtation.

"Maybe you all can stop talking about me like I'm not here," I say.

What I really wanted to say was, if I was a goddess, I would have struck my father dead long ago, but to even whisper those words would result in punishment. Knowing my luck, someone would overhear me.

"Yes, enough of that Aksel, how many times does she have to deny you before you stop your advances?" Astrid kicks sand at her brother.

"Never. The moment I stop may be the moment she finally gives in," he chuckles.

"Please. Stop." My brother pinches the bridge of his nose.

"How about we go for a swim?" Astrid uses my back to push herself to standing before turning around and offering me her hand. As soon as I am on my feet, she pulls me in for a hug.

"I missed you, my friend," she whispers into my ear.

"And I you."

I go to remove my clothes before reality slams into me and I stop. Espen is by my side immediately.

"You can wear my tunic if you wish to swim."

"And how will you explain to Father why you are wet and smelling of the ocean?"

"You let me worry about that."

"No, Espen."

He opens his mouth to argue but instead walks over to Aksel, leaving me in peace with Astrid.

"I love that he knows when to speak and when to shut the fuck up. I wish it would rub off on Aksel."

I couldn't control my burst of laughter. It felt good to laugh and so freely. My mother, brother, and I might steal a few giggles here or there, but anything more than that would be frowned upon. My father not only leads with an iron fist, but he believes fiercely in Stoicism. Showing any type of emotion was a weakness.

"He certainly does. My father has no idea how well he has trained him."

"What is the old saying? Where wolves' ears are, wolves' teeth are near."

"I could picture Espen as a wolf. One that would put Fenrir to shame. At least in size, he would not take part in ending the world."

"No. He would do anything in his power to save it."

That is a characteristic I really envy about Espen. He is fearless when it comes to the people he cares about. I can't count the number of times he has come to my defense, even when I beg him not to. I am not weak, but I am certainly not fearless.

"Are you ever going to tell me why you won't swim?"

It is a simple question, but the answer is far from simple. The anguish in my gut almost overcomes my control, but I swallow it down and force a smile.

"Maybe one day."

"You don't need to hide from me, Bryn. Your secrets, your fears, are safe with me."

I plop back down on the sand next to her. She is carefree and at ease watching Espen and Aksel play fight in the surf. Why was I the only one who couldn't just... relax?

"I know I don't, it's just... I forgot what truly being safe feels like."

"You will remember. A change is coming."

I have known Astrid for years and never heard her speak like this. Usually, she gives me advice. Tells me not to give up, but this? This was a premonition.

"How do you know?" I turn to her, hoping to make eye contact.

Her smoky gray eyes meet mine. "Just like you won't tell

me why you won't swim, how I know is my secret. Trust me."

The urge to ask her all the questions claws at my throat, but since she has respected me, I owe her the same courtesy. Instead, I move closer and lean my head on her shoulder. She, in turn, wraps an arm around me, filling me with her warmth. I hadn't felt the chill in the air until now.

"I can't promise there won't be more heartache, but I can promise you will find your purpose."

Now she was sounding like an Oleg the Wise, and I was starting to question how well I really knew Astrid and Aksel, but how well do we really know anyone? We put on a front of what we think everyone wants to see and what is proper while our true selves watch from the shadows. I pray for the day I can just be me. No matter the consequences.

My mother's whistle echoes over the water, calling us home. It would be beautiful if it wasn't bringing us back to the pits of Niflheim. Astrid pulls me in closer, providing a final moment of comfort.

"Please don't let it be so long before I see you again."

"I will do my best."

With that, we part ways, and my brother and I prepare for what may await us at the palace. We return the same way we departed, through the servant's quarters on the back side of the property. No one asks any questions, let alone acknowledges our presence.

We are edging close to our rooms when my father's voice booms out.

"Brynja Skye Hallstrom!"

Fear radiates through my bones, but I don't dare show it on the surface. I turn around calmly and bow at his feet.

"Where have you been? Whoring yourself all over town?"

Thankfully, my face is hidden from view as I bite my lip to fight back the tears. "Never, Father."

Which is true. I have never and would never. I feel my brother kneel next to me before I hear his words.

"She was with me, Father. I would never allow her to be disrespected."

"I don't remember acknowledging you, Espen. You can remove yourself from my presence and find your way to bed. You have training early."

I don't need to see Espen to know he's wavering. I can feel it in the way the air shifts between us. He's torn—should he obey Father's command, or stay and protect me?

"Leave them alone, Ragnall. They left the palace at my request."

Seemingly this evening's fight was going to be a family affair.

"And why would you allow Brynja to leave the palace grounds when you know she is on strict orders to stay put?"

"Because it is ridiculous to order her never to leave. She is a woman and not only that, she is your daughter, or have you completely forgotten?"

I can feel the rage pouring out of my father. How he can be so angry at someone he used to love and adore and how did all of that change based on one person? A person he only knows by name and reputation.

"I haven't forgotten anything but clearly you have," he says, striding toward my mother. Espen locks eyes with me and shakes his head. He knows where my thoughts have gone, and I have no doubt his are the same.

"Why don't we stand up to him? Together," I whisper.

"Do you have a death wish, sis?"

"Father may be a lot of things, but he wouldn't kill us."

Espen's cognac eyes turn to midnight as fear, stark and vivid, cloud them. I've only seen fear in his eyes one other time.

"I wouldn't be so sure," he says. His unbridled reaction mixed with the tone of his voice has a knot of fear and anger battling in my gut.

The sound of skin hitting skin echoes down the hall, and I am on my feet and at my mother's side before I can stop myself. Fiery rage pulses through my father's facial features, but I refuse to turn away. Most often I bend to his will, but I've also taken his wrath. I can and will continue to do so in defense of my mother and brother. I may have lost my father and a lot of myself—not by choice, it was taken from me—but I will not lose what is left of my family.

He reaches for me, and I am all but ready to face my punishment when my brother steps in front of me.

"No, Father. You will not touch them."

"I can and will because I am the king. You all would not be here if it wasn't for me."

"I didn't know you made and birthed these children alone. You must be the talk of Frigga herself."

He rears back to strike my mother again at the mention of the Goddess of Fertility, but my brother reaches out and places his hand on his shoulder. The small gesture stops my father in his tracks and his eyes are now focused on Espen. I remember the days when a similar gesture from my mother would have him melting into a puddle.

"Sir King, please. We are your family. Will you not treat us as such?"

For a small glimmery moment, I see the father I used to know. The one with compassion and undying love, but it is gone just as quickly as it came as he laughs.

"A family? You are traitors who I graciously let live here because I must keep my reputation intact if we are to win this war."

"So, in order to win a war, you start a war within your own walls?" Espen asks, no longer holding back.

"I'm not the one who started the war." My father begins to walk away, tired of what I'm sure he deems a beneath-him argument.

"No, Father. You did. You may not have started the war that wages beyond these walls, but you did start this one. How do you not see that we are not the same as Sigvard?"

"Do not say his name in my house!!" He closes the distance between them so they now stand toe to toe.

"Ragnall my love, please," my mother pleads, her voice slick with worry.

"Your begging is as pathetic as your attempts to fool me. You have no love for me as I have no love for you. Guards take them!"

As we are dragged away, I watch my hope trail behind me. Through everything, I clung on to hope that things would change. My father would remember who he was, who we were, and we would be a family again but here we are, thrown away like garbage...again.

I wonder how long it will last this time.

WHAT FEELS LIKE AN ETERNITY LATER, I lie on the cold hard floor of the cell I have been tossed in. I have no idea where my mother and brother are, but I can only assume they are in the same situation. There is a makeshift bed in the corner made of old straw, but the coolness of the floor feels pleasing against my back. I'm also at just the right angle so that out the window I can catch a glimpse of the night sky. Watching the stars twinkle and dance, I try to remember what life was like before all of this. When things were simple and... beautiful.

Midgard had always been an exquisite realm filled with many cities and all types of people. Created for us by the gods themselves, we couldn't have asked for a better place to call home. Of course, we have had our share of disagreements, threats of war, but my grandfather always found a way to fix it. He was a true king. A king who would rather perish then let anything happen to any of his people. When my father first took over, things remained prosperous for several years, until it wasn't. He became more stern, less caring, and when the rebellion started, he completely snapped. Anything good left in my father vanished. I prayed to the gods, to Odin the All-father, to come and return order. To show my father what true power looks like, but my prayers have gone unanswered. If I could go to Asgard myself and beg for his help, I would, but very few humans can cross the Bifrost Bridge. It is a realm only for the gods and their closest relatives.

My other option is to run off to my mother's homeland of Thora. Nestled between the great rolling hills of Rosvin and the snowy peaks of Kaldir, it is the place I truly call home. Yes, I could run off and hide anywhere, but with a large army at my father's disposal and the fear of death hanging over everyone's head, it wouldn't take them long to find me or for me to be turned in by a terrified citizen. In Thora I would be protected by its loving people but at cost far too high to pay. Which is why I have never left, he rules over all of Midgard. I dream of it often, but on top of putting everyone else's life at risk for my own, I could not leave my mother and my brother.

When we were children, we used to visit Thora every other weekend to spend time with my mother's family. Espen and I would play in the fields of tall swaying, whispering Wasp flowers with our cousins and forget anything else existed. When nightfall came, we would catch lightning bugs and tell them our wishes. Once set free, if your lightning bug made it back to Odin, your wish would be granted. I wished for years for a baby sister, not only for companionship but for support against Espen. He always beat me at everything. That is, until the other day.

My truly favorite part of the trip was seeing Mormor Thorsson. Having never met my father's mother, she was the only elder woman left to teach me the ways. Mothers are meant to care for you and prepare you for womanhood, while Mormor is responsible for teaching you the traditions and lifeblood of the family. On my eighth birthday, she presented me with a beautiful, handcrafted leather book. Inside contained all the stories of the gods handwritten by Mormor. I read the stories over and over again, memorizing not only every aspect of the tales, but the way Mormor swirled her letters. In the back of the book, mere pages from the stories of the gods' greatness, were the stories of her family. They took me back thousands of years to when the world was created by Odin and his brothers using the corpse of Ymir, the first giant and Odin's grandfather to create everything we know today.

She taught me everything, and I never got to say goodbye to her. To give her a proper burial. I don't even know what they did with her.

"Brynja?" a voice whispers, but I'm not sure if it is a delusion. I want to answer, but if the wrong person hears me, I will be down here even longer.

"Brynja, can you hear me?"

I attempt to move, but my body is somewhere between frozen and searing, so I call out from my position. "Hello. Who's there?"

"Praise the gods. Brynja it's Orn."

Orn has been a part of my father's guard since I was a young child. He has always done his best to look after me. He can only do so much without causing suspicion, and I am grateful for all the risks he takes.

"You can't be seen down here!" I do my best to sound stern but my lung capacity is limited.

"It's my turn to be on duty, so do not fear. Can you move? I brought you some tea and an apple."

Just the thought of moving makes me cringe, but the promise of warm tea is encouragement enough. I crawl over to Orn and position myself so I am leaning against the wall closest to him. He kneels down and places the apple in my lap, covering it with a cloth before handing me the small cup of tea. My hands tremble, but the moment the warm liquid meets my lips, it brings a calm to my body.

"I hate seeing you like this."

"What of Espen and Mother?"

Orn looks away, his body rocking in discomfort. He knows there is no sense in hiding anything from me but still tries to spare me.

"Out with it."

"Your mother is in a similar state to your own, but your brother he is… worse for wear." I attempt to stand but Orn puts a soft hand on my shoulder. "There is nothing you can do for him in your current state. I have provided him with what I can and will keep eyes on him until morning."

"If he worsens, you tell me immediately."

"Of course, Princess."

Orn rarely calls me princess, not due to lack of respect,

but because we view each other as family. He only uses the term when he wants to make a point. The point now is he will not let my brother die alone in a cell. Tears well in my eyes and I am not sure if they are for Espen, my mother, or myself. Orn wraps his hand tighter around my shoulder.

"Brynja, I promise this will not be how it ends for your family."

A small laugh of disbelief escapes my lips. "Do not make promises you have no control over, Orn."

His eyes meet mine, and he does his best to give me a kind smile. "You are right. I do not have control, but I do know that the gods would not let your story end like this. With no... purpose."

"Plenty have perished without purpose. Don't pretend otherwise."

"Are they meaningless? Or are they due to people fighting for what they truly believe in? If that is not purpose, I don't know what is."

I had never thought of war in that sense. To me, it has always been the acts of men trying to prove who has the bigger ego and the most power. I guess I truly am just a princess with only the views my father allows me to have. No matter how hard I try to break free from his shell, there is always another layer waiting to constrict around me.

I make a promise to myself at that moment. If I get out of this cell, I will learn everything Espen has to teach me. I want to be prepared for whatever this world still has in store for me. Wait...

"Orn?"

"Yes, Brynja?" He releases my shoulder so he can lean against the wall closest to me.

"Will you help me learn about what is truly going on outside of these walls?"

"Your father really keeps you in the dark, doesn't he? Tell me what you know and I will start from there."

"All I know is there is a rebellion led by a man named Sigvard and that my father says they have no chance of winning against his superior army."

Orn chuckles with amusement. "His army may in fact be superior, but that means nothing if you can't find your enemy."

"What do you mean?"

"Drink your tea, sweet Brynja, and let me tell you."

CHAPTER 2

"The rebellion started long ago. As an idea, a dangerous idea. The king never deemed it a serious threat. That it would never become more than just an idea. How could slaves be anything more than slaves? That was his first mistake. One of the first things you need to always remember, Brynja, is never underestimate your opponent."

I nod as I set my tea aside and take a hearty bite of the apple. The sweet juice drips down my chin and once again, I remember what life was like when things were much simpler. Just Espen and I, in the field of whispering wasp flowers sharing an apple. Orn's voice brings me back to my current harsh reality.

"By the time the king realized it was serious, it was too late. Sigvard had escaped with a horde of men at his side and a thirst for blood. Within two days, he slaughtered a quarter of the king's army and increased his own with every slave he set free."

"Is it known how Sigvard became a slave?" I ask, my curiosity about my father's enemy piqued.

"There are many tales, but no one knows where the truth lies and fairy tales begin."

I can't help the small smile that pulls at the corners of my mouth. "That sounds all too familiar," I mumble.

Orn's pats my leg in comfort before continuing. "The king, of course, was furious. He sent more and more men, but Sigvard was always one step ahead of him. He has not been able to locate Sigvard or his army of slaves turned free men, and every day a new head arrives at the palace. A constant reminder the king is losing."

"No wonder he is so furious all the time." I take the last bite of my apple. Orn signals for me to give him the core and the cup. I do as requested, and he tucks them away somewhere inside his tunic.

"I'm convinced that is the only emotion your father knows anymore. He is not the man I first met, either."

"What was he like?" I want to be sure the father I remember from childhood wasn't just a dream I concocted.

"He was... kind and cunning. Witty and firm in his loyalty. Most importantly, he was fair. Anytime someone came to him, he found a way to come to a fair outcome."

"What changed him? I know it wasn't just Sigvard. Something else had to have happened."

Orn shuffles uncomfortably. He may break some rules when it comes to me and my family, but his loyalty, his oath to the King and to this land, is something that lives within his soul.

"Being king is a heavy burden. One he refuses to share

and, as a result, each day he loses more and more of himself."

For a fleeting moment, I feel bad for my father. He had everything a man could want, yet he let his own pride set fire to the things he loves the most. I manage to stand and walk over to the straw bed in the far corner of the cell. It takes every ounce of strength I have remaining not to collapse onto it in a heap. Instead, I gingerly crawl upon it and curl myself into a ball. Tears paint my cheeks as I weep for all the things I have lost and all the things yet to come.

THE CLANG of something solid against metal pulls me from sleep. I attempt to roll toward the sound but every part of my body protests.

"Time to get up, Princess. The king requests your presence tonight for an important dinner."

I have no idea how long I have been asleep or even how long I have been down here, but I would rather stay put than attend this "important dinner." His treatment of us is one thing, but having to put on a show and pretend like we are one big happy family adds insult to injury. The door to the cell opens, which would normally fill me with joy, but at this moment, dread courses through my veins.

"Get up or I will make you get up."

The guard's threat is not empty, and I am too hollow to fight back so I do as ordered.

He escorts me all the way back to my room and, even after closing the door, remains outside. I don't know what is more disheartening, the lack of escape or the lack of trust. Thankfully, a friendly face is waiting inside my room. Thyra.

"Your Royal Highness, I was so worri—"

My arms are wrapped around her before she can finish speaking. She hesitates before pulling me into her warm embrace. I want to cry all over again but refuse. I am here now with my friend and will enjoy it.

"I'm fine, Thyra." I pull back looking into her sea-green eyes.

"I don't know how fine you are. You have been gone for three days," she says, tucking a strand of hair behind my ear.

Three days? Father was livid.

"Truly? Three days?"

"Yes, ma'am. I have prepared you a bath and some food should be up shortly."

I am surprised he is letting me eat with such an important dinner tonight, but if he didn't, he would have to explain my growling stomach and paleness. The bathroom is thick with steam and smells of lilacs and peppermint. Thyra helps me peel off my clothes before guiding me into the tub. The hot water brings welcome relief to my body as I slide beneath the surface. Just as I always do, I hold my breath as long as I can before resurfacing. Thyra reaches for the soap, but I shake my head.

"Let me soak awhile first. Please, Thyra."

She nods and leaves me be. As much as I enjoy having such a beautiful bathroom, I miss the baths Mormor Thorsson used to give. She would fill a large wooden tub with water so hot my skin would tingle upon entering. Then she would scrub me with a soap Vikings have used for centuries. Made of animal fat, ash, and lye, it could remove the strongest of odors. It also had the ability to lighten hair, but if my hair got any lighter, it would be the color of snow. Once done, she would braid my hair and wrap me in fox fur. Together we would sit in front of the fire and she would tell me stories. It was in those moments I felt like a true Viking.

Everyone in this realm, in Midgard, is a Viking. We just hail from different cities and have varying lives. My family is the sole royal family in Midgard. It was our purpose... once. To keep peace. To keep order. For everyone. My brother has been training to take over for my father since he was a child. I am expected to marry and carry on the bloodline.

Traditional Viking women get to be so much more. They have... freedom. I wish I could tell them all how lucky they are even if it may not seem that way. Money is nothing when you don't have your freedom. This gets me wondering what kind of challenges they do face. Mormor Thorsson was always so happy, but I'm not naïve enough to think everything was perfect. Perhaps one day I will find out.

Thyra knocks softly and awaits my permission before re-entering the room. Being my friend and servant is not easy on her, but she manages it with grace. Without another word, she tends to me. We learned a long time ago how to understand each other in silence. I would love to converse with her, to hear all the stories she has to share, but you never know who is listening and what their intentions are.

Once I am out of the bath, she begins the task of getting me ready for dinner. I take a seat at my vanity, and she places two color palettes in front of me. One is fiery red and the other is cobalt blue. Given the last few days, red is the only appropriate option. It doesn't matter what my father does to me, my fire will never, ever go out.

"Red please, Thyra."

"Excellent choice, ma'am. You have the perfect gown to match."

"You always know exactly what I desire," I say, giving her my best smile.

"It is my job, ma'am." She winks before sitting behind me to braid a portion of my hair.

"Any word of my brother?" I can't stop myself from asking. I need to know he is okay.

"He is alive, but that is all I know."

The male and female servants are not allowed to speak to one another. Not only that, their quarters are separated and the only one with a key is my father. He does not want any of his servants getting pregnant or creating families. It just makes problems. According to him, anyway. I think he just wants to deprive everyone of any sort of pleasure. To make them as miserable and lonely as he is.

Once my hair is braided and curled, Thyra moves on to my makeup, red eyeshadow with black smoky edges and lips the color of blood. It perfectly matches the gown. Given to me by my mother, it is deceiving from the back. Long velvet sleeves and a high neck give a sexy yet traditional feel. The front dips low between my breasts before snaking tightly around my waist and flowing to the ground. The final touch is a single red ruby hanging from a long silver chain. It stops just at the swell of my breasts. My father will be angry, but when is he not? I might as well make him angry and feel sexy as the goddess Freyja doing it. He also expects me to be broken. To beg for forgiveness. I will ask for forgiveness, but I will never beg and I will never break.

When I step out of my bedroom door, the same guard is still in place. His eyes fall to my breasts briefly before he quickly walks away. I scan the hallway for any sign of my mother and brother, but there isn't another soul in sight. I say a silent pray to Odin and follow my guard toward the dining hall. Several voices I don't recognize permeate through the dining hall doors. I wonder who my father is parading us in front of now.

As the doors swing open, my presence is announced.

"Princess Brynja Hallstrom"

Immediately all eyes are on me. I pass over the faces I don't recognize and focus on my brother. Dressed in all blue, he looks utterly handsome except for the bruises and cuts all over his neck and face. To the unfamiliar eye, they would not be noticed. His servant has done an excellent job concealing them, but no amount of effort could hide them from me. Physical wounds aside, there is no denying the pain in his eyes. Whatever father did to him this time was exceptionally cruel. I move toward him when I feel my mother's hand on my shoulder. Our eyes meet and I recognize the same pain in her eyes. The one blessing is I do not see any visible wounds on her.

"Mother." I bow my head.

"Brynja, please come and meet our guests."

I follow her over to the two unfamiliar families standing with my father. I search my memory for any indication I have met them before but find nothing. The moment my father lays eyes on me, his expression clouds with outrage. He is quick to catch it, tucking it away for later as he wraps a cold, unloving arm around me.

"I would be honored for you to meet my daughter, Brynja," he says, pulling me in tighter to his side.

All of them bow. They are beautiful families. One consisting of a mother, a father, and three children, two girls and a boy. The boy is the oldest, by my guess, with the youngest girl appearing to be around ten. The second family has a mother, a father, and one son. Everyone is dressed in matching blue outfits that are simple yet charming, leading me to believe they are of higher standing. I also clearly was meant to wear blue. This is some sort of matching affair. I wonder why Thyra gave me the option.

It hits me like a lightning bolt. This isn't just some sort of matching affair; it is an arrangement for me.

"Brynja, are you going to keep ignoring our guests?" My father grips me tighter than necessary. Words must have been spoken, but I was too lost in my own mind.

"My apologies, Father. I am so pleased to meet you all," I say, bowing my head in honor.

The young man from the smaller family steps forward, and a flicker of anxiety courses through me.

"This is Arik," his father says from behind him.

"Princess Brynja, it is my honor and pleasure to make your acquaintance." Arik takes my hand in his as he kisses the top before kneeling at my feet.

I don't need to see my brother to feel his fury raging behind me. The entire room is being swallowed up by it, along with the uneasiness brewing in my gut. I need to say something, and as much as I don't want to, it would not be wise to aggravate my father any further.

"Arik I'm delighted to meet you. Please stand, you do not belong at my feet." I turn my hand palm up to help him. Once on his feet, he guides me over to the dinner table. He pulls out a chair and I reluctantly sit. Everyone else finds their place, and I am grateful to have my mother and brother on either side of me. The three fathers take their places gathered around the head of the table. Arik sits directly across from me.

He is a good-looking boy.

Man.

Thinking he was a boy was highly inaccurate on my

part. He is at least comparable in age if not older. His hair is darker than most Vikings, appearing more brown than blonde. I would call it golden chestnut, but the darker color makes his crystal blue eyes all the more striking. His hair is pulled back, and his beard is trimmed close to his face, much like my brother prefers. Espen has never been a fan of the long, full beard. He finds it irritating and too much of an upkeep. My father prefers this as well, claiming royalty should always keep a fresh, clean appearance. I say it just adds to the separation and makes us easy targets.

The siblings from the other family are all stunningly similar. They have the same ashy blonde hair and green eyes, except the older sister. Her eyes are a deep blue, like the color of lapis lazuli. The soft ivory color of her skin gives the appearance of innocence, but I sense that is not accurate.

The servants pour everyone wine except the youngest sister and leave us to finish dinner. The room remains uncomfortably silent until my father's voice fills the room.

"I apologize for Brynja's appearance. I hope this will not sway you from our arrangement."

"No need to apologize, Your Majesty, it changes nothing." Arik's father smiles, holding up his wine.

"Wonderful, then the only thing left to discuss is who shall be married first."

First? What in the boar's backside was he talking about?

I look over at my mother, who is feigning a smile and hasn't said a word.

"I believe the future king should marry first. Would send the proper message to your people that your family is strong and the rebellion is nothing more than a thorn in your side," the other man says, his eyes scanning over his three children, who appear just as uncomfortable.

Father nods, but he is not happy to have the rebellion mentioned inside his house. Thankfully, the man was smart enough to know not to refer to their leader by name. I wonder if he would throw him into a cell.

"Mm, yes, I agree."

"Do I at least get to know my bride-to-be's name, or shall it be kept a secret until the wedding day?" Espen asks, his voice thick with ridicule.

"Espen!" My mother surprises me. She may dislike this arrangement, but she is never disrespectful to guests.

"Apologies, Mother. It's just Brynja received an introduction, and I did not. It is rude to…" He pauses and looks at his future bride, hoping she will fill in the blank.

"Isa. My name is Isa, Your Highness."

"It is rude to Isa. Please accept my apology, Isa. I am Espen."

"Well, now that we are all introduced, Espen and Isa will be married next month. Brynja and Arik the month after."

"Your Majesty, may I make a suggestion?" My mother's soothing voice rolls over the table.

"Of course, my love."

I shudder at the use of the word love, but my mother smiles like it has touched her heart.

"I believe we should spread them out more. Putting them so close together will look suspicious and I would like time to make Brynja a wedding dress."

My father's lip twitches, but before he can argue, Isa's mother chimes in.

"That is a beautiful idea, Your Majesty. I would like to do that as well. Perhaps you can help me?"

"It would be an honor. I propose we postpone the

weddings until after the autumnal equinox. To allow time for the dresses to be made."

All eyes turn to my father. I expect him to put his foot down or to at least argue, but instead he says, "That would be wonderful. I do prefer not to be out in the heat."

"Then it is settled!" Arik's father claps his hands together just in time for the food's arrival. My mother and Isa's mother exchange glances and I wonder what they have said without speaking. Perhaps she will tell me later. For now, I must smile and act like the perfect daughter.

Too many hours and not enough food later, I am finally back in my room. It's not that an inadequate amount of food was served; there was enough to feed the entire city, but I didn't want to bust the seams of my dress.

"Thyra, please get me out of this."

She gives me a small smirk before responding, "Yes, Your Royal Highness."

She doesn't even have a sleeve off me when there is a knock at the door. My heart sinks. I'm not ready to be banished back to a cell. I need my bed. My body needs the bed. Thyra leaves my side to answer the door. The door swings open, and as I ready myself to face my fate, my mother swirls in like the warm tropical breeze she is.

Without hesitation, I dash into her arms.

"Oh, my sweet Brynja, please accept my apologies."

"For what, Mother?"

"For this arranged marriage. I tried to stop it, but you know how your father is. The best we could come up with was a way to delay it."

"We? So, you do know Isa's mother." I pull away so I can look into her eyes.

"Not well, but Mormor Thorsson tended to her father, so she feels forever indebted to me. She is a good woman and has a lovely family. Both families are. If these marriages do happen, you and Espen will not be treated poorly."

"Don't make promises you don't hold the key to, Mother."

This gets a smile out of her. "Always so witty," she says, brushing my hair off my forehead.

"What happened to her father that Mormor Thorsson had to tend to him?" I knew Mormor was a lach, her healing prowess was well known and sought after, but she didn't share many stories. She believed that physical vigor was meant to stay between the ill and their gods.

"He was very ill. Deemed to be taken any day but she nursed him back to health. He lived another six years," she says, leading me over the small table near the window. Her smile deepens at the memory of Mormor as she takes a seat in the far chair.

I manage to find my own smile as I sit across from her. Thyra brings over two glasses of wine and a large piece of almond crown cake. I had been eyeing the cake all of dinner but never took a piece. My mouth is watering at the mere sight of it.

"I had a feeling you wanted a piece, so I arranged for us to share one."

Thyra turns to leave, but I grab her hand. "We can all share."

"I am flattered by your offer, Your Royal Highness, but I mu—"

"Thyra, this is not a request. Sit," my mother instructs her.

She does, but her eyes remain locked on her skirt. I hate she lives in constant fear and I am partially to blame. I place my hand gently on hers.

"Please enjoy this moment with us. I need a good memory after so many bad ones lately."

A faint light twinkles in the deeps of her eyes. "Then a good memory we shall make."

I hand her my wine glass and pick up a fork. I have gone long enough without sweetness in my life, I will not deny my tongue any longer.

CHAPTER 3

I awaken to cries and chaos throughout the palace. I have no idea what took place overnight, but it has everyone in a panic. When I step out onto the balcony, it is made clear.

Thirteen heads are on spikes lining the walkway up to the front door. I recognize most of them as my father's guard, including the one who escorted me just last night. Sigvard and his men never miss an opportunity to enrage my father and instill fear into his men. What is left of his guard are in a panic, trying to remove the ungodly scene. Beneath one of the men is a woman on her knees, crying. I can only assume it is his wife. The guards are allowed a life of their own due to the risks they take. Servants are nothing more than a necessity according to my father, who is also nowhere in sight.

I walk to the kitchen in search of breakfast and, hopefully, Espen. Knowing my brother, he is looking to make up for every ounce he didn't consume during our three days in confinement. He takes his physical robustness very seriously.

Just as I suspected, he is in the far corner of the kitchen, a plate stacked with food in front of him. The morning chef adores him and cooks him whatever he wants. This adoration isn't just due to his charm, I believe she finds him handsome.

"Is there enough to share, or is that all for you, dear brother?"

"You are the only one I would even consider sharing with, plus you are going to need it." He smirks.

"Oh? And why is that?"

"We are training today."

This has me astonished. We just got out of trouble and he is ready to tempt fate again.

"Espen, do you really think that is a good idea?"

His smile deepens, touching the corners of his eyes. "Yes, sis. Father is gone and he will not be back anytime soon."

My father rarely leaves the palace, and when he does, it's only to attend to important matters. That combined with the thirteen heads outside must mean far worse things are happening in the realm. It also means Espen and I will be the least of anyone's worries.

"Where did he go?"

"To the battlefield. So, sit. Eat, and let's pray he never returns."

I eat not even half the amount Espen does, and I am so full I wasn't sure my shieldmaiden would fit. I manage to stuff myself into it and hurry out to Vildmark. Even with Father gone, this is the safest place to train. As soon as I break through the brush, Espen attacks me. I try to make a dash for my sword, but it is too far away and I'm not fast enough. I have to use my arms to block. I take the first blow on my bracer, but if the second one would have been delivered at proper speed, my arm would be in bad shape. Espen froze, the blade mere inches from my skin, causing goosebumps to form. His control is unparalleled.

"You have to be ready at any given moment for an attack, Brynja. If you can't get to your sword, you must find another way. What else can you do?"

I don't even give myself time to think, I just react. I slap Espen in the face as hard as I can. He doesn't budge.

"I give you points for reaction time, but really? A slap?"

"I don't know! It's just what I did. I'm not a warrior like you."

"That is your first problem. You think you are not a warrior when you are. We have trained since you were little and you have a sword, don't you? You even dream of being a warrior."

"Steel alone does not make a warrior," I tease, finally able to grab mine from the ground.

"You are right. Just the possession of a sword does not make you a warrior, but I know you are one. You just have to believe. Trust yourself and trust me."

I want to make a clever remark but instead I just nod my head. If there is one person I trust in this world, it is Espen.

"Back at it again, are we?" I hear my favorite voice call from behind me. Showing up right on cue, just as we discuss trust.

"Agnarr! Did you come to get bested by my sister?"

"The day I get bested by Brynja is the day the gods no longer favor me."

I attempt to hold back my laughter, but there is no stopping it. My brother joins me and the look on Agnarr's face only fuels the fire.

"You can laugh all you want, but I speak the truth."

"I'm in agreement with my sister. Why of all people would the gods favor you?"

He clears his throat and looks away. Seemingly Agnarr was not joking. I may not know him well, but I do know is he has two main traits. Oathbreaker and fool-born. Serious is not something he ever is. At least not in front of me.

"What is it?" Espen asks Agnarr, also noticing the change in his behavior.

He shakes his head. "It is nothing. Let us train."

Espen and I exchange glances. We both know it is not nothing, but we also know pushing him will solve nothing. Instead, I hold my sword and stand ready in front of him. I rejoice in my training, forgetting who I am and becoming whatever I want. Right now, I want to be strong and unstoppable. The smirk returns to Agnarr's face, alerting me that the asshole has returned.

"Let's dance, Princess."

His sword strikes mine as he moves forward aggressively. Normally I would back away, attempting to keep space between us, but today I hold my ground. Our swords grind together as the space between becomes almost nonexistent. I catch him shifting his weight to put more pressure on me, but when he tries, I back off, causing him to stumble forward.

"Good, Brynja!" Espen bellows enthusiastically.

"Enjoy the moment, Princess. You will never beat me."

"Maybe not today, Agnarr, but I will one day."

"Ha! I do admire your resolve. Again!"

Before I can even take another breath, his sword is bearing down on me. He strikes repeatedly, cutting side to side, but I match every blow. What I am not prepared for is when he thrusts at me. The blade is long and it is not easy to defend such a move. He pretends to stab me several times before he sticks it into the dirt.

"Let me help you, Princess. Espen, come live the highlight of your day and pretend to be me."

Espen shakes his head but does as Agnarr requested. In turn, Agnarr comes around behind me, pressing our bodies together and wrapping his hand around mine. There is a brief zing of hot electricity and a flash of the same vision from before. It comes and goes so quickly I barely have time to process it.

"The thrust is not as dangerous as it seems. All you need to do is redirect the attacker's momentum," Agnarr says, bringing my focus back to the present.

Espen thrusts his sword toward us and Agnarr guides my hand sideways, pushing Espen's blade out and away.

"You see, he has put all his weight forward. If you force him to the side, he is off balance and must react. Understand?" Agnarr is actually teaching me something. He usually just... kicks my ass. Befuddled, I nod. "Now, you work with Espen. I came here for the show and perhaps a nap, not to be a part of it."

"But you always end up a part of it," Espen chuckles.

"I can't help it that I'm the better warrior out of the two of us."

There he is. Loki must have temporarily cast a spell on him. Before I can think about it too long, Espen begins his attack. He uses his height and strikes down from high above. I have to extend my arms at the cost of some of my strength.

"Do not overextend yourself, sis. Force me to come to your level."

"And how exactly do I do that?" I grunt against his weight.

"Just as I have used my height to my advantage, use yours."

Even though it seems foolish, I have no choice. My arms are tired and do not stand a chance against him in this position. Using the new technique Agnarr taught me, I push his blade away and crouch low. From here, I realize I have easy access to his middle and legs. I strike once on his chest plate before spinning and striking him again on the back. Espen falls to the ground in an overdramatic display.

"It looks like all the years of training are finally paying off, you have slayed me."

I'm not sure who laughs louder, me or Agnarr. Espen is right about one thing, everything I have learned is finally... clear. He has been trying to teach me how to wield a sword since I entered womanhood. His reasoning was he didn't have enough hands to fight off all the men gawking at me, and since Father couldn't care less, he insisted I learn to handle it. This eventually blossomed into me becoming a full-fledged warrior. It has been a slow process, but it seems the fire is finally starting to burn. Espen is back on his feet, ready for another round. So much for him being slayed.

"Take him down a couple more pegs, Princess. Maybe I won't have to hear him brag for a while," Agnarr calls, looking way too comfortable lying in the sun on his fur.

"How about I take you both down a few pegs?"

Agnarr just chuckles but Espen is brimming with pride. "About damn time you got out of your head. Now. Attack me!"

A war cry unfurls naturally from my chest as I charge Espen. My first strike is high, bringing his focus up. When he attempts to counter me, I spin around to his back. I manage to hit him twice before our swords clash together again. He gets two excellent hits on me, leading us into a full-fledged battle. Our swords meet again and again, the clang of metal sounding louder with each collision until we are both breathless. My arms burn as if lava is running through my veins. The sword is not light to begin with. Having to wield it nonstop makes it feel heavier with every impact, but I refuse to give up. I move in closer, striking him in the chest once more before pushing my butt into him and flipping him over my back.

I immediately drop my sword, not caring anymore, and fall to the ground beside him. Neither of us speak as we struggle to catch our breath. There isn't a cloud to be seen, the sky reminiscent of the lake behind Mormor Thorsson's house. Every visit I swam in the lake. I loved the feeling of being weightless with nothing but the heavens above. Perhaps if I focus on the heavens now, I can see Mormor. Instead, Agnarr's shadow appears over us.

"Did she just flip you on your ass?" He grins at Espen.

"She did indeed, and I'm convinced my soul will never return to my body."

"You don't need to placate me, brother," I say, rolling my eyes and myself away from them.

"I'm not placating you, Brynja. I didn't know what was happening until I was on my backside and my soul was looking back at me."

How my brother has maintained such a wonderful sense of humor will never make sense to me. I am, however, thankful for it. Agnarr helps him to his feet before coming to help me. I push his hand away, wanting not even the slightest reason to be in his debt.

"Come, Princess. You knocked him down, now let me help you up."

I can't stop the smile tugging at my lips. I beat my brother. Agnarr is proving he can be kind—when he wants to be. And Father... Father is finally gone. This is the best day I've had in a long time. Thank the gods, it was needed. I reach for Agnarr's hand. The moment our hands meet, electricity courses through me and the world shifts.

I'm falling from the heavens. Nothing is around me but sky and swirling wind. I try to scream but no sound comes out. Even if it had, there is no one around to hear me. I'm alone and falling to my death. I close my eyes, prepared to embrace my fate when I'm caught. Warmth and safety surround me like a bubble. I open my eyes to see who saved me, but I can't.

I'm back on the ground with Espen's arms wrapped around me. Agnarr is gone and my heart feels like it's going to come out of my chest.

"Bryn! Are you okay?"

"What happened? Where did Agnarr go?"

"He thought he hurt you, so he went for help."

"From who?" I remove myself from Espen's arms and find my feet.

"Mother, of course."

"Why would he get Mother and not you?"

"If you think I would leave your side while you are unconscious and leave you with Agnarr, you definitely have a head injury."

I chuckle. "Apologies, brother, you are right."

I graze my skin with my fingertips, seeing if I can feel any remnants of what just happened, but there is nothing. I've had vivid dreams for as long as I can remember but have never experienced them like this. These... visions feel real. How can I go from here to there so seamlessly, and what is Agnarr's part in it? That is the third time now that we have touched and I've had some sort of vision.

My mother comes flying around the corner like a butterfly in the breeze.

"Brynja! Are you okay? What happened?" She pulls me into her arms.

"I'm fine, Mother, they are overexaggerating."

She holds me out at arm's length and looks over every bit of me. Softly, she skims her thumb against my cheek before offering a subtle smile.

"You do look alright. Filthy but alright. Come. All of you. Let's get cleaned up and have dinner on the balcony tonight."

A DELICATE BREEZE whispers around us as we enjoy dinner on the balcony. Espen can't eat fast enough while Agnarr seems to be just moving food around his plate. I can't remember the last time he joined us for a meal. He always seems to have other plans but always manages to attend our training sessions. The more I think about it, the more I ascertain that Agnarr is somewhat of a mystery. I don't ever remember meeting his parents, or any sort of family for that matter. After all these years, how can that be?

"Not hungry, Agnarr?" I ask, starting the conversation as discreetly as possible.

"Not really, Princess, but I don't want to offend Her Majesty." He looks over at my mother.

"Eat what makes you happy, Agnarr, you will not offend me. Believe it or not, Espen used to hardly eat anything. Nothing was pleasing to his palate."

Espen stops mid-chew when he hears his name. "What?"

"Oh nothing, darling. I just hope you are at least tasting what you are consuming."

"Apologies, Mother. Training has made me famished."

My mother grins before taking a bite of her fish, and I return my focus to Agnarr.

"What is your family like during dinner time?" I ask.

Everyone pauses like I have asked a question that is highly inappropriate for dinner conversation. Seemingly I am the only one who is in the dark about Agnarr. I should not be surprised. They have been friends since they were boys, and my mother knows all. Much like Mormor Thorsson. She learned from the best.

"I seem to have overstepped. I was merely curious. I feel as I don't know you as well as I should, Agnarr."

He clears his throat before meeting my gaze. "My life and my family are none of your business, Princess." His tone has changed drastically along with the color of his eyes. The Agnarr I am familiar with has returned in full force. Normally I would let this go and just excuse myself, but I am tired of letting people walk all over me. My mother blessed me with her strength, it is time I use it.

"If that is the case, then you can remove yourself from my life and my family."

"Ha!" Agnarr says loudly, throwing his head back.

"Sis, please, thi—"

"Espen no need. I see where your loyalty lies. Mother, please excuse me."

I walk away before any more words can be exchanged. It was improper for me to do that during dinner and in front of my mother, but enough is enough.

My room is quiet when I return except for the faint

sound of the curtains fluttering in the breeze. Freyr, the God of Good Weather, has blessed us with a shorter winter and favorable temperatures. Normally this time of year a fire would still be required. Thyra must have returned to her quarters, which is unfortunate. I was hoping to spend some time with her but I understand. She needs her peace and freedom to be herself as well.

I strip down to my underwear and grab my book from the nightstand. Repositioning the chaise lounge so it is near the window and facing out, I make myself comfortable. The mix of crisp air and a magical story transport me to a different time. That is, until someone knocks. Can't I even get a moment's peace? Placing my book down I go over to the door.

"Who is it?"

"It's Espen. Can I come in, please?"

I ponder saying no, but I am also interested in what he has to say. Surely, he didn't come here just to scold me, at least I hope not. I do, however, make him wait several moments before opening the door. He is in his nightclothes as well and holding a mug in each hand. The bruises and cuts are now clearly visible on his face without the makeup. My heart hurts for him briefly before I remember I am upset with him.

"Well, can I come in or not? I brought your favorite wine."

"Wine in mugs? How classy, Espen."

"I figured less questions would be asked if I was carrying two mugs assumed to be filled with hot chocolate instead of two glasses of wine." He gives me his best half-smile.

I step aside, letting him enter. He walks straight to the

table near the window and sets down the mugs. I remain by the door, unsure how to take his presence. Espen and I have always been bonded. Not just because we are brother and sister but by something even deeper. I have no way to describe it or even understand it myself except to say it is a blessing from the gods. We have our disagreements, of course, no relationship no matter the strength goes without conflict. He has just always been my... unshakeable counterpart.

"Please come sit with me," Espen says, his voice gentle and quiet. He has already taken his place in one of the chairs. The desire to hesitate still pulls at me, but wanting to find out what really occurred at dinner is more appealing. I sit across from him and begin sipping on the wine he so graciously brought.

"Agnarr is so—"

"Please don't tell me you came here just to make excuses for Agnarr."

"I didn't. There is just something I want you to know and understand about him. It does not excuse his behavior, but it may make you more...amenable."

"I would be more amenable if he treated us the same, but he does not."

"It is because he is jealous of you."

"What?" Shock tumbles through me.

"He is jealous of our relationship, to put it more accurately. He has no family, Bryn."

"What do you mean, he has no family? He wasn't just placed here by Odin. So, what happened?"

"They are all gone. He lives alone on what is left of their land. They were all killed."

My gut drops to my feet as a feeling of guilt and shame overtakes me. Mormor Thorsson always told me never to judge someone without knowing their circumstance. Agnarr is just so infuriating sometimes.

"How?" I swallow hard, wondering if I will be able to handle the answer.

"It pains me to say this, but I don't know. He won't tell me." Espen looks away, his mug trembling in his hand as he attempts to take a sip.

Curiosity joins my other emotions. All these years Agnarr has never told Espen what happened to his family. That seems very odd. No. No. Remember Mormor's words. I can't judge what I don't understand. I try to ponder how I would feel if my family were taken from me, and the mere thought sends a stab of grief tearing through my heart.

"I can't fathom how much pain it must bring him."

"Nor I. It is why I have never pushed him to talk about it, but what I do know is he wasn't so... callous prior to losing them."

"Did you ever meet his family?"

"Just his mother. Once."

"What was she like?" I ask, hoping to shift the conversation to a happier topic.

"She was very kind. Much like Mother. Had the same eyes as Agnarr but with more... softness."

We exchange tentative smiles. "Are you telling me all this so I will forgive you for siding with him?" My smile unintentionally widens.

"I was just trying to stop an argument from happening at the dinner table. You know how much it displeases Mother. We already have so much anger in our lives."

Espen is right, but now I have more questions and I need answers. I am tired of feeling like I am always left in the dark. If it's not my father, it's the rebellion. If it's not the rebellion, it's Agnarr.

"You are right. I should have held my tongue."

"I understand why you didn't. Agnarr knows how to press buttons."

"Well, it's time for me to press his." I walk to my closet.

"Bryn... what are you doing?" Espen asks, his eyes following my path.

"I am going to go see Agnarr."

"Now!?" His eyes widen in surprise.

"Yes, now." I pull on a pair of trousers and a fur vest.

"Okay, you've had too much wine. Let's get you into bed."

I grab my mug of wine off the table and drink the remainder, followed by what is left in Espen's mug.

"Or you have just lost your mind. Come, Brynja, this is not funny."

Just a few steps from the door, I pause and turn back to Espen, who is still standing next to the table, dumbfounded. I hate to see my brother so distressed, but I won't sleep. I already have too much on my mind.

"I'm tired of feeling like the little princess left in the dark. I'll be back before sunrise."

And I walk out.

CHAPTER 4

I have never been inside Agnarr's home, but the land and surrounding area are very familiar. Espen and I used to pretend his sweet forest cottage belonged to a dark elf and we were hunting him. It was how Espen taught me the beginnings of being a warrior and I didn't even know it. To me, it was just a fun time with my brother. I debated briefly sneaking in a window and scaring Agnarr, but I'm not in the mood or proper attire for that. A knock on the door will have to do.

Much time passes, and just as I am about to knock again, the door finally opens. Agnarr is in nothing but his linen underwear. I can't stop myself from blushing. It's one thing to see him on the beach in just his trousers, it's another to see him all sleep rumpled in next to nothing.

"Brynja? What the Niflheim are you doing here?" His voice is a mix of concern and annoyance.

"I need to talk to you." The wine swims in my veins. It's

not enough to inhibit my judgement but enough to make me bold.

"And that had to happen now? I was just about to go to be—"

Before he can finish, I push past him into the house. If I didn't do it, we would waste another ten minutes bickering before he finally closed the door in my face. The inside is not what I expected. Everything is neat and organized. He even has a small vase of plum starling flowers sitting on the windowsill.

"Did you come here just to tell me to get out of your life again, Princess?"

"Don't even start with me, Agnarr. You have said far worse things to me…"

He goes to speak but quickly changes his mind. At least he seems to figure out he will not win this battle. Or at the very least he is letting me win this round.

"Why do you hate me?" I ask the question that's plagued me for years.

His eyes grow large with disbelief. "I don't hate you. It's j—"

"I swear to the gods if you call me Princess one more time, I am going to strangle you."

"Is that a challenge?" He raises an eyebrow.

Of course, he would rather brawl than exchange words. That would require too much effort. Fine. He wants to play, I'll show him how I play. I walk toward him until we are directly in front of one another.

"If you want me to strangle you, I'd be happy to fulfill that fantasy." I graze my nails around his neck. Goosebumps form in their wake.

"Real funny, Princ—"

Before he can chide me again, I wrap my fingers around his throat and squeeze. "Don't call me princess."

He places his hand over mine, squeezing gently. "You are in dangerous waters, Prin... Brynja."

"Really? Then how come I don't feel the least bit scared?" I walk forward, forcing him against the wall. "You, Agnarr, are the one who should be scared."

I wrap my second hand around his throat but only apply light pressure. His eyes darken with displeasure and his nostrils flare. I know he is going to counter me, but for the moment, I enjoy my dominance over him. I attempt to press my knee between his legs to gain even more control, but he spins us around and slams me into the wall.

"You must stop."

"Why? You going to kill me?" My eyes lock with his. He smirks.

"I would never."

I roll my eyes and do the only thing I can from this position. I knee him in the balls. He crumbles to the ground coughing, and I laugh. I have wanted to do that for years but never had the... balls. I push away from the wall and head for the kitchen, but I only make it a few steps before he yanks me to the floor. My shoulder hits first, sending a stinging shockwave through my neck. I attempt to reach up and rub it, but Agnarr is on top of me immediately with my arms pinned above my head. Rage pulls at the edges of my control but seeing the tears in Agnarr's eyes from the knee makes me smirk. He bites his lip and looks away.

"I am going to let you go and you are going to walk out of here and never look back."

"Aww, are you mad because you are losing?"

He bends down, his mouth touching my ear. "It doesn't look like I am losing, Princess."

In one fury-invoked swoop, I flipped our positions. Pressing my lips to his ear, I say, "I wouldn't be so sure about that."

From that moment, it is a frenzy of limbs. We roll back and forth. Knock over chairs. Slap. Throw elbows. Until we end up back where we started with him on top and both of us gasping for air.

It's at that moment I realize we have been touching this whole time and I didn't have a vision. I reach up and place my hand meekly on his chest to see if I can force anything to happen. He stills. The muscles beneath my fingers are taut and slick with sweat. The ache for a man I felt days earlier resurfaces, but I quickly push it back down. My desire does not understand this is not the same. She just knows she is extremely thirsty. I pull my hand away in embarrassment and attempt to slink away, but Agnarr will not let me.

He places my hand back on his chest with both of his over mine. Slowly, he drags my hand from the mountains of his chest down over his abs. I'm trying to understand what is happening when his hand trails down my arm and around my elbow. We are too close to avoid eye contact, but what I see now is far from displeasure. It's desire. Fiery, all-consuming desire.

His lips meet mine and my body quivers. They are soft and harsh all at the same time. I suck his bottom lip into my mouth before biting it. He isn't the only one who can be soft and harsh, but we have already proved that.

"You drive me insane, Princess," he growls, throwing my hands above my head and pinning them again.

"And you are a swollen arse."

"You want a swollen arse, I will give you one."

Using my wrists, he pulls me toward him and rocks

back on his heels, so I am face down in his lap. Before I can think, let alone protest, he swats my arse so hard I see stars.

"That is for kneeing me in the balls."

I want to speak, to say something snippy, but my brain can't form a word, let alone a sentence. It's like a rabbit trying to outrun a wolf, the only thing it can focus on is the escape. He lands another slap that stings so hard I can feel it in my toes.

"And that is because I can." His voice is deep and gruff.

The sting of his hand mixed with the gravel in his voice sends mixed messages all over my body. My head is screaming *what the fuck is happening*, but my desire is screaming for him to rip my clothes off. I have to get out of this, and fast. I bite his leg. The moment his grip loosens, I get to my feet and dash for the door. I stay on my feet for all of three seconds before tripping over a chair and ending up right back on the floor.

Agnarr appears over me, but instead of pinning me down again, he offers a hand. Tentatively I take it.

A vision swirls around me. This time I am not alone. I am standing back-to-back with... Agnarr. I can't make out what is around us, but we are filthy, holding swords tainted with crimson. I try to find focus. To bring my full consciousness into whatever this is, but I can't. All it does it send me barreling back to reality.

When I open my eyes, I am still on my feet, but Agnarr is holding both of my hands.

"What in Hel's underworld was that?" he asks.

"You saw it too?"

"If you mean your eyes turning white and you looking like death, then yes, I saw it."

I shake my head, "No I..." I stop as the look of disbelief washes over Agnarr's face. Aggressively, I pull my hands away. "Never mind. You never believe me anyway. It was a mistake coming here." I turn to leave, but he spins me back around.

"Why did you come here, Princess? Truly."

I ignore the anger over him still calling me princess and just let the words bubble up. "To get answers. To try and understand why you treat me how you do. You aren't the only one who has secrets. Who lives with desires for something... more. Yet you purposely find ways to diminish me. Why? Just tell me why and I will leave and never bother you again."

His eyes meet mine, but I can no longer read the emotion behind them. "Because you are a constant reminder of everything I don't have."

The anguish of his words threatens to shatter the last threads of my control. I imagined Agnarr saying a lot of things. That was not one of them. Even though Espen told me he lost his family, I never expected him to admit his true feelings. To me.

"Agnarr, I'm sorry."

"I don't need your sympathy. There are reasons I never speak of it."

My mind spirals with a million more questions, but I know better than to push my luck. I never presumed I would get the answer I already received, which leaves me with no words. Instead, I just stand awkwardly in front of him.

"You going to leave now, Princess? Or are you going to let me finish what you started?" He closes the distance between us.

"And what exactly did I start you... horse's arse?" It was a terrible insult, but I'm lucky I came up with anything.

"This battle of forbidden lust."

Did he just say lust or is the wine swirling in my brain turning this encounter into the complete opposite of its purpose?

"Or would you prefer to call it hate lust?"

There was that word again, but do we really hate each other? Or is there something else beneath the surface that we have been blind to? Mormor always said there is a fine line between love and hate.

"So do you hate me?"

He throws his head back with laughter. "Out of everything I just said, you managed to focus on the one negative word." He moves closer until our bodies are touching. His lips hover above where my neck dips into my shoulder. "I do not hate you. You drive me mad, but hate… no, Princess."

Goosebumps have formed in the wake of his hot breath against my skin. My head involuntarily falls to the side as he trails kisses up my neck.

"Do you know how many times I have fantasized about kissing your lustrous skin?"

"You did an impeccable job keeping it a secret. What other secrets have you been hiding, Agnarr?"

"That shall be the only secret you are blessed with today," he says. I can feel the smile on his lips as he drags his teeth along the outer edge of my ear.

My hands find his chest again. I hold my breath, waiting for a vision to take me away, but I am locked in this moment. I have had my share of men but none with a physique like Agnarr's. His chest is nothing but sharp edges covered by velvet soft skin. If I hadn't grown up by his side, I would swear he was a descendant of the gods. My fingertips trail down every perfect, glistening inch and as they journey, I can feel his heart hammering against his chest. When I reach the crest of his shorts, one of his hands grabs my wrist while the other pulls back on my hair.

"Prin..." He squeezes his eyes closed. "Brynja, if you go a tomme farther, I will be undone and there will be no stopping me. So, this is your final warning. Do you truly desire me?"

The way his voice trails off surprises me. Agnarr has always been self-confident. Why now, when he has full control, does he question? I inhale a deep breath, fighting the hold he has on me.

"Agnarr, look at me."

The smoldering flames of desire dancing in his eyes take my breath away. I can only hope my eyes are giving him a window into the maddening pleasure searing in my bones, but I must speak. He must hear my words.

"I desire you in more ways than I care to admit. The look in your eyes alone could be my undoing, so please put me out of my misery."

The flames in his eyes burn brighter and his grip on my hair tightens. He pulls me close. My hand curls up the back of his neck while my other digs into his chest.

"I thought you would never ask."

His demanding lips caress mine, but I am eager to satisfy them. Parting my lips, I rouse his passion with my tongue. He lifts me from the floor effortlessly and presses my back into the wall. I snake my legs around his waist, pulling him into my frame. His arousal greets my thigh, and I can't stop the gasp that leaves my lips.

"Prepare yourself, Princess. We are just getting started," he says, his lips still pressed to mine. I swallow his words like they are the only thing that will keep me alive.

He pulls off my fur vest with no effort, and I am quickly reminded I have no undergarments on. In my haste to leave, I never even considered putting them on. His hand cups the swell of my breast as he uses his thumb to encircle my nipple. My limbs quiver. The ache of my desire is now front and center, and there is no pushing her back down anymore. She will stay until her thirst is fully quenched and I no longer wish to fight with her.

I reach back and release my hair, letting it fall free around my face. He buries his nose in my neck and takes a long inhale. A groan from deep in his chest unfurls and finds a new home inside my body. It's a sensation I have never felt before and the only thing I can do is bite down on his shoulder. In response, he rips off my trousers and presses into me. The sole thing separating us now is the thin linen of his shorts, damp with his arousal.

"You have no idea how badly I want to lose myself deep inside of you."

I want to tell him to do it. To let us both get lost, but we have played this cat-and-mouse game for far too long and I'm not ready to give it up just yet. I kiss his lips softly and his grip eases just enough that I can slip away.

I walk over to the front of the bed and turn back to face him. He is watching me but has not moved from where I left him. His chest heaves with lust, but he has no clue I have barely scratched the surface. I pull my tunic over my head, baring myself completely to Agnarr. He takes a step toward me, but I hold up my hand. He pauses.

"You said it yourself. We are just getting started."

I lie back on the bed, making myself comfortable. He rearranges his feet, still respecting my wish for him to stay put but allowing him to release the inescapable desire to join me. Starting at my neck, I trail my hand gradually down my body, making sure to take my time at my breasts. My eyes stay on his as I make my way to my cunt. I am wet and ready, but I force myself to focus on my clit first, circling it slowly. Agnarr falls to his knees.

"I thought you were driving me mad before but that was nothing. This is pure torture. I beg you, Princess, let me suckle on your sweet cunt."

Seeing him on his knees is enough, but hearing him beg has me teetering on the edge. I bite my lip. Hard. The effortless pain mixed with the taste of iron reels me in enough so that when I push my fingers inside, I don't cum instantly. Agnarr bites his lip as he rakes his hands through his hair. The fusion of Agnarr's desperation and my fingers has my body humming with a rapture I have never known. Who knew torture could be pleasurable?

Agnarr collapses on the floor, his hands pulling at his hair. "Please, for the love of the gods, stop this madness."

A smirk finds my lips. I'm enjoying this way too much, but I am far from done. "Take off your shorts."

Agnarr rolls over so he can look at me. Probably to check if I am serious. I continue to work my fingers as I lick my lips. He removes them and returns to standing. He is a sight to see. Indescribably handsome. A sculpted mountain. His hair is wild, along with the look in his eyes, and I want him more than Loki requires mischief. I have one more thing in mind.

"No—"

"Enough. You've had your fun. Now it is my turn."

Instantly he is on top of me, reclaiming my lips. His tongue sends shivers of desire racing through me. I wrap myself around him, wanting to be as close as possible, but he has other ideas. His tongue goes from pleasing my mouth to pleasing my cunt. His mouth tantalizes my clit with a hot possessiveness as moans melt from my lips. He is everything sinful and I don't want to be a good girl ever again.

Just when I think I can't climb any higher, he slides two fingers inside of me and his other hand slides down my taut stomach.

"I have never felt or tasted anything sweeter," he says, his lips humming against mine. I press into him, needing more, and he chuckles alluringly. "Have we tortured each other enough? Are you ready to feel my true desire, Princess?"

"Yes please, Agnarr."

"Fucking Hel, you are a siren."

He goes to turn me on my side and before I can stop myself, I yell, "No!"

He looks at me, stunned. Before the moment can be completely ruined, I pull him back on top of me and slide him inside my wet and waiting pussy. His lips find mine once again and we swallow each other's moans. I expect him to go hard and unruly, but he does quite the opposite. His touch remains light and painfully teasing. He fills me completely and pulls out slowly so I can feel every vein and... piercing? Whatever it is, it's like little ridges of pleasure.

Together we find a tempo that binds our bodies together, causing wave after wave of ecstasy to throb through us. Hearing my name leave his lips is something I never want to forget even though I have a feeling tomorrow things are going to look very different.

CHAPTER 5

It doesn't take long for Agnarr to drift off to sleep, but to me, it feels like hours. As soon as the high wore off from my climax, a million questions filled my mind. The top one is how I will explain to Espen why I am coming home in Agnarr's shorts instead of the trousers I left in. Even still, as much as I want to regret it, I don't. My desire has been quenched beyond my wildest dreams and maybe, just maybe, things can be different between Agnarr and me.

I return to the palace before the sun and the servants awake from their slumber. I slide quietly into my room, thinking I can finally breathe, when I see my brother asleep on my bed.

"Hels," I mutter, dashing to my dresser before he stirs. Stuffing Agnarr's shorts into the back of the drawer, I put on a fresh pair of trousers and head to the bathroom.

"What happened to the pants you left in, Brynja?"

His voice is dark and inquisitive, causing the hairs on my arms to stand up. It is not that I am afraid of my brother, it's that I'm terrible at lying to him.

"I fell in a puddle, and they got all wet and dirty, so Agnarr gave me a pair of shorts," I say, my back to him. I hear him move off the bed.

"That sounds awfully nice of Agnarr, and if that is true, why hide them in the back of your drawer?" He moves closer to me.

"You know what would happen if Father found them. Three days in confinement would be child's play."

I don't have to see him to know his entire body stiffened at the thought. I take the opportunity to dash into the bathroom and end the conversation. Thyra will not be up for several hours, so I make my own bath.

When I sink beneath the surface, I relish the aftermath of my time with Agnarr. My swollen lips, the dull pain on my arse, and the raw ache between my thighs. It may come with regrets, the biggest one never being able to experience it again. Even if he was willing, which I doubt, my brother would never let it happen. Agnarr may have talked a big game, but I'm not foolish enough to believe everything that came out of his ruttish mouth. It was a means to an end.

When I finally emerge from the bathroom, I am surprised to find my room empty. Espen never lets things go—but he'll wait and make me pay for it during training. With Father gone, we will train every day until he returns. So much time is stolen from us, we take advantage of every moment when we can.

I am about to go to the kitchen when Thyra appears in my room.

"Good morning, Your Royal Highness. How did you sleep?" Her question is thick with sarcasm.

"I did not." The words spill out before I can stop myself. Thyra's eyes grow wide with curiosity. A part of me knows I should not be sharing any of my secrets, but she is one of two people in this world I trust.

"Apologies, ma'am. Would you like me to draw a bath?"

"I already bathed, but thank you, Thyra."

Now I truly have her attention. I hardly ever draw my own bath, not out of lack of ability but because that is our time to chat uninhibited. She knows I am trying to hide something.

"If you would bring up some breakfast, that would be wonderful. Include enough for yourself if you have not already eaten."

She bows and exits the room. While she is gone, I check both of the attached rooms. They are empty, but to ensure that does not change, I lock them from the inside. Even with Father gone, there are still many among the staff who cannot be trusted. She returns with a tray of food for me and coffee for two. If there is one thing that Thyra thoroughly enjoys, it is coffee, and the staff is not allowed any. It is too great of an expense, according to my father, so the servants are only given tea.

I dig into my food, eating much like Espen does, as Thyra slowly sips her coffee. I didn't realize how famished I was until the first bite touched my lips. Thyra sits quietly, unbothered by my lack of manners, as I finish the plate and pour myself a cup.

"You aren't even going to ask?" I say, the first taste of coffee already awakening my tired shell.

"That would not be appropriate, ma'am. I—"

"No one is listening, Thyra, I made sure of it."

"Oh, thank the gods. Please tell me what happened. It was killing me not to ask."

"You certainly didn't show it," I chuckle. "You might want to set your coffee down. I would hate for you to burn yourself."

She sets her cup down without hesitation and leans in close.

"I had sex with Agnarr last night."

The shock of my words hit her with a force as strong as a bull. "It is a good thing you had me put my cup down. I'm almost certain I would have dropped it. You and Agnarr?! How?"

"I went to his cottage last night to have words about the way he speaks to me, and one thing led to another…"

"That still does not explain how speaking leads to spanking."

How did she know he spanked me? Just the thought has me jump as if he had struck me again. Thrya's eyes go wide.

"Did he truly spank you?"

Her question has me feeling slightly embarrassed. Should I have not allowed that, let alone enjoy it as much as I did? I did knee him in the balls, after all. I had earned it. Just didn't expect the tingling pleasure it would provide.

"He did indeed." I do my best to keep my voice steady. Thyra picks up a napkin and fans herself.

"You must tell me everything. I have only read of such things in novels. Please let me live through you."

My embarrassment completely fades away, and a devilish grin takes its place. "I will tell you everything you wish to know."

Thyra and I are lying in the sun on the balcony when Espen calls from the doorway. I knew he would return but I had hoped not so soon. At least it was after my retelling of last night's events. Thyra quickly busies herself with my hair, regardless of Espen being well aware of our friendship.

"Come, get up. Get dressed. We have some training to do."

"Can't we skip it for today, Espen? I am tired and the sun feels good."

"Why are you tired, dear sister?"

Not wanting to answer the question, I quickly change into my training gear. Thyra finishes my hair, tying it into a tight braid around the base of my skull. Before I can leave, she offers me some parting words.

"He won't give up until you answer him, Brynja. You know how Espen is. Might as well be honest with him."

There are so many things I want to say but none of it matters because she is right. I owe Espen the truth. Whether he will approve or not.

The moment I step into Vildmark, I can hear the clash of swords. No. Not today. Please tell me he did not just show up like every other day. Sure enough, when I break through the clearing, Espen and Agnarr are training.

"About time you showed up, Princess. Was starting to think you were being a coward."

I choke back my agitation and instead grab my sword. "And how would you know someone is a coward, Agnarr? Personal experience?"

Espen laughs under his breath, but they continue to battle. Agnarr clearly wants to say something but focuses his attention on the task at hand. I sit and observe, memorizing all the moves I can. I feel my strength with the sword is finally adept, I just need to improve my footwork and bring it all together.

Agnarr attempts to strike Espen but as he does, Espen makes a move similar to mine yesterday. Espen is taller, so his arse presses squarely into Agnarr's chest, but the results are the same. Agnarr lands flat on his back.

"Who knew a move my sister randomly came up with could be so effective," Espen chides, reaching down to help up Agnarr. He takes his hand and gives Espen a good slap on the back once he is back on his feet.

"It is the only move she is effective at, brother."

Hot anger boils out of me before I can stop it. "That is not what you were saying last night."

My words stop Espen dead in his tracks as both of their eyes land on me. Espen looks rattled while Agnarr appears to mirror my anger.

"This isn't funny anymore. Tell me what fucking happened last night!" Espen demands.

"Fucking is exactly what happened."

"Brynja, have you lost your damn mind? Don't listen to her Espen." Agnarr attempts to put his hand on Espen's shoulder, but he immediately brushes it away and focuses on me.

"Bryn, are you telling me the truth? Did you two..." Espen can't even bring himself to say the words, so I do him the favor of only nodding. He turns back to Agnarr, clutching the hilt of his sword so tightly his knuckles are white. The death-awakening yell he releases echoes across Vildmark as he charges at Agnarr. When their swords clash, I swear I see a spark.

"You promised, Agnarr!" Espen yells, bringing his sword down again.

"And I kept that promise for ten years, brother. Now she is a grown woman. With desires that must be met."

I don't know what is more embarrassing, them talking about me like I am not here or that some promise was required for Agnarr to keep his hands to himself.

"It is not your job to meet those needs. Ever."

"I think she would beg to differ," Agnarr says, looking at me and winking. This only manages to make Espen even angrier. He starts violently slashing at him as if he were truly on the battlefield and panic settles into my gut. I knew my brother would be upset but not like this.

"Espen, I don't want to hurt you." Agnarr does his best to defend or dodge my brother's unrelenting blows.

"I cannot say the same!" Espen says as his blade makes contact with Agnarr's shoulder, casting a line of blood. I can no longer sit by and watch this scene unfold. I dart in between them with no regard for myself.

"Stop! That is enough!"

Espen drops his sword and falls to the dirt. I can hear his cries before I can see them. Sitting next to him, I curl my fingers around his chin and force him to look at me. His face is a meld of blood, dirt, and tears. I have only seen my brother cry one other time. Something much more is going on here. Agnarr sits so his back is directly behind Espen's but without touching him. He shifts between looking at the sky and down at the dirt.

"This isn't just Agnarr's fault. If anything, I am the one at fault. I went there unannounced and uninvited. Please do not let my... lack of judgment ruin your friendship."

Espen laughs and jerks his face out of my grip.

"She still defends you when you treat her so poorly. What's next? Will you abandon me for him, dear sister?"

"Espen, you hear my words," I say, doing my best to control my temper. Of all the people in the world, Espen is the last I would ever abandon, and for him to question that makes me want to slap him. "There are two people in this world that I trust. You, Espen, are one of those people. Abandoning you would be like losing a part of myself."

His eyes meet mine again, tears pooling around the edges. "There are only two people in this world I trust as well, but now... I am only left with one."

He gets up and storms off without his sword and without looking back.

Agnarr and I remain in silence until I can no longer hold the guilt eating at my heart. "Apologies Agnarr, I didn't think he would take it so poorly."

"Ha! You did that on purpose. You wanted me out of your life. You succeeded."

Agnarr pushes off the ground and steps away to leave but I will not let another person walk out on me. I grab his wrist and force him to sit back down and face me.

"You can be furious with me, but I will not lie to my brother, and you will never be out of our lives."

"What don't you understand, Brynja? Without his trust, we are nothing. I am nothing."

"Over one night with me? That is not significant."

"But the promise was," he says, shifting away from me.

"And what was this ridiculous promise?"

His eyes meet mine, and there is an odd pain behind them. Something I have never seen from Agnarr before. He is always so stoic or full of humor or desire...

"That I wouldn't let my feelings for you take control."

I must have teleported to another realm because there is no way Agnarr just said he has feelings for me. That or this is another one of his cruel jokes.

"Very funny, Agnarr. What was it really?"

He runs a hand across his face before pinching the bridge of his nose. "For how clever you are, you are blind to what is right in front of you."

He leaves without another word, and I am left with an overwhelming amount of guilt.

I remain in the dirt for a long time, trying to untangle my feelings. After a while, I decide the only thing that makes sense is to train. I don't need Espen and Agnarr. I take my sword and go into the forest. Much like me, the forest appears beautiful on the outside but inside holds many secrets. Secrets that can only be discovered if you are patient enough to endure the silence.

Surrounded by the towering trees with their looming secrets, I turn each and every one into the enemy. I run, strike, dash, twist, and turn my way around, leaving no tree unscathed. Thunder shakes the earth from above, and I take it as a sign that Odin approves. Torrential rain pours down, but I am not fazed. The forest will bow before me. The ground beneath my feet is slick, requiring great effort not to fall. Holding the hilt is increasingly difficult from the mix of rain and burning pain in my muscles. I take another strike as fast and as hard as my body can manage when the ground beneath my feet melts away and all my momentum carries me backward.

I hit the earth hard and tumble like a rock downward. I grab desperately at anything in view to stop my progress, but I can't get a good hold. As my body picks up speed, every rock, stick, and tree I hit is like slamming into a cement wall. Turning myself vertical, I attempt to use my feet to halt my progress, and that is when I see it.

The ground ahead ends and drops off into oblivion. Panic sears through my veins as I claw at the earth behind me. Nothing is working. As I inch closer and closer to my death, I say a final prayer to Yggdrasil, the Goddess of Life, to not let me leave Midgard this way. My legs go over the edge and just before I close my eyes, I see a thick tree root snaking over the edge and down toward Niflheim. I hold my breath and reach out.

The moment my hands make contact, I clutch hard as my body slams to a halt against the side wall. All the air is knocked out of my lungs and every muscle screams, but I have stopped plummeting. There is nothing but darkness below. The chasm is so deep not even light can reach its depths. Using what is left of my strength, I climb up the root to the edge and collapse flat on my back.

Eyes closed, the cool rain is now a welcome relief against my burning skin. It also makes it impossible to tell where the rain stops and my tears begin. I survived but this is far from the end. I have to make it back to the palace and I must make amends with Espen. Agnarr too. How terrible would it have been to have died and those were our last words?

Pushing myself into a kneeling position, I look around for the best way out. If I must attempt a climb back the way I came, I will, but it is a last resort. Just when I think I will have to tempt fate again, there appears to be a path around the far corner of the chasm. It is hard to tell in the rain and from my position, so I compel myself to stand and begin walking.

A throbbing pain soars up my leg, blurring my vision. I grit my teeth and force myself forward. As I get closer, I fear I am wrong when I finally see a clear path. If I wasn't in so much pain, I would fall to my knees and thank the gods, but I would not be able to get back up. Once again, under the canopy of the forest, I find a stick to aid me. Relieving some of the pressure off my leg helps considerably, and I am renewed with a small sense of strength.

When the palace walls finally come into view, relief washes over me. I never thought I would be happy to return here. As always, I return through the servant's entrance, but unlike usual, many surprised eyes fall upon me, including Thyra's.

"Your Royal Highness, are you alright?"

I give Thyra a tight smile before my body collapses out from under me and the world goes black.

CHAPTER 6

I am back on the battlefield, war raging around me. The snow-white sword I remember from before is in my hand. We exchange a surge of power, and I have never felt stronger in my life. I raise both arms, bringing an aura of energy around me, and just as the release is ready to spring from my fingers, I fall backward.

My eyes fly open as I gulp air into my lungs. I am no longer on the battlefield but tucked safely into my bed. My nightgown is stuck to my skin from a thick sheen of sweat and everything aches. The memory of the previous day comes flooding back, and briefly, I am back at the edge of the chasm. I claw at the sheets for safety when I feel a set of hands on me.

"Your Royal Highness, it is alright. You are safe."

I try to see through the panic, but it is quickly overwhelming me.

"Ma'am, look at me!"

My eyes dart to the voice, and Thyra's sweet face comes into view. She reaches out and cups my cheek with her hand. "You are safe, I promise. Breathe."

I take several deep breaths and feel my body unwind. She leans me back against the headboard and hands me a glass of water. I sip slowly, realizing how thirsty I am.

"You had us quite scared, ma'am. I wasn't sure I would ever see you again."

"What do you mean? How much time has passed?" I ask, confused.

She places a gentle hand on my lap. "It has been four days."

Four days? I was unconscious for four days after a fall. It couldn't have been that bad. I force myself out of bed and to the mirror in the far corner of the room. Thyra is never farther than a few inches from my side. The moment I see my reflection, my hands clasp over my mouth in dismay.

There is hardly an area of my skin that isn't covered in bruises, including a large one encircling my left eye. Blood is crusted and flaking off around my hairline and what I can see of my right leg is covered in bandages.

"Her Majesty and His Royal Highness were so concerned with your condition they have gone to Thora."

"Thora?" I ask with both confusion and concern. "Why?"

"Her Majesty went to request the Lach of Thora come here to heal you. She was not... satisfied with the royal one. His Royal Highness refused to let her travel alone."

I do not blame my mother. The lach my father hired knows nothing of ailments or herbs. He relies more on mechanisms, something she has never believed in. A different kind of guilt washes over me.

"How long ago did they leave?"

"Just yesterday, ma'am. They should return by sundown tomorrow."

I bite my lip, fighting back tears. I have caused so much pain with such a stupid act. Desperately, I wish I could take it all back. Thyra moves closer and cups a hand around my shoulder.

"Don't cry, you are awake, and they will be so happy upon their return. Come. Let me bathe you."

There are so many words I wish to say, but I don't have the strength. Instead, I just follow her into the bathroom.

The hot water stings, bringing tears to my eyes, and I can't stop the hiss that escapes my lips as I lower myself into it.

"Apologies, ma'am. I added sea salt at the request of Her Majesty to reduce your swelling and remove any toxins."

"It's currently removing my soul from my body," I say as my arse finally reaches the bottom of the tub.

Thyra smiles gently. "Glad to see you are still in there. We were all worried."

"Then please stop calling me 'ma'am' and tell me what has happened since I returned."

She looks around cautiously before scooting her stool closer. She begins by gently washing away the dirt and dried blood from my arms. The water is already a disgusting shade of sepia.

"Everyone was in a panic. Trying to figure out what happened and who did this to you. Espen was convinced it was Agnarr, but he swore on his life it was not. Her Majesty had to calm Espen down. I assume you... told him?"

I nod, not wanting to speak or react before the story is complete.

"Once Espen was convinced Agnarr had no part in it

and three days had passed since you collapsed, they decided to go to Thora. Agnarr has been standing guard outside of your room. He has not left for a moment."

My eyes meet Thyra's. "Agnarr is here?"

"Yes, Brynja. He has refused to leave."

"Why?"

Her eyes meet mine and a blanket of comfort envelops me. "I believe you already know."

Once I am clean and in proper attire, I take another look at myself in the mirror. The bruises seem even more prominent now that the blood and dirt have been washed away. There is a deep gash on my leg, which explains the pain I felt on my journey back. It has since been properly cleaned and tended to, and the pain is now bearable. I have hidden all my injuries with clothing, except my face. I want Thyra to put makeup on me, but I am sure Agnarr has already seen me. There is no sense in hiding.

When I open the door, Agnarr is sitting on a stool barely big enough for him. It looks like it could give out at any moment. He is quickly on his feet, but the moment he sees me, he stops dead. He reaches out for me briefly before stopping himself, unsure what to do. So, I decide for both of us. I wrap my arms around him and place my head on his mountain chest. He wavers before embracing me and resting his head on top of mine.

"I'm so sorry, Brynja." His words are quiet but potent.

"I'm the one who is sorry. I should have never told Espen like that."

"Let us both just agree to be sorry and thank the gods you are alive."

I nod against his chest in agreement, not wanting this moment to end. His strength and warmth are slowly renewing me. He pulls away, his gaze once again taking in my injuries.

"What in Midgard happened? Were you attacked? We couldn't find you or your sword anywhere."

Shame blooms in my chest. How can I possibly tell him what happened without sounding like a fool? I remain silent, hoping we can forget about what happened, but he removes me from his arms so he can look into my eyes.

"Brynja..."

"It was of my own doing," I say, looking away.

"What. Happened."

"I was training. Using the trees as enemies when the ground gave way. I tumbled down and almost ended up dead at the bottom of a chasm. I am already humiliated enough, please keep your harsh comments to yourself."

What he does next completely astonishes me. He kisses me.

Not just a brief touching of his lips to mine. A sensual, feverish kiss. One that leaves me absolutely breathless...

"I know I have spoken many harsh words to you," he says, his lips still touching mine. "But the mere thought of you dying makes my blood run cold."

"Fairly certain you already had cold blood." I smirk.

"Now who is using harsh words?"

"I am just so horrified, Agnarr. I nearly kill myself trying to train, and now my mother and brother are—"

"Brynja, calm yourself. It could have happened to anyone. It was raining, the ground was soft. Let us not focus on the regrettable but on what is favorable. Come back to bed. You need your rest."

I attempt to protest when Agnarr scoops me up into his arms and carries me. As much as I want to journey to Thora, my body will not be able to handle it, and once under the covers, there is no denying it. My eyes are instantly heavy. Agnarr turns to leave but I grab his hand.

"Stay. Please. Your presence and warmth are an immense comfort to me."

I am being very vulnerable with Agnarr, but he has done the same. There is no hiding anymore. At least not at this moment.

Without another word, he crawls into bed beside me. He lays stiffly like a wooden board, keeping his hands to himself until I pull an arm around me. As I melt into him, he does the same and I quickly drift off to sleep.

WHEN I WAKE, my position is exactly the same, but Agnarr is shirtless and breathing softly. I rotate in his arms so I can face him. The peace of sleep has brought a softness to his features, making him younger and less... tormented. There is a scar on his jaw I have never noticed before. It runs along the edge before curving up close to the corner of his mouth. Perhaps that is why he is never clean-shaven, an attempt to keep it hidden. The question is, is he hiding it from others or himself?

I press my lips gently to the scar and string a line of kisses up to where it stops beside his mouth. Agnarr's hand lands at my lower back.

"Don't tempt me, Princess."

"You are back to calling me princess?" I roll my eyes.

"You are a princess, are you not?" he asks, his lips now on the edge of my jaw. "A sultry captivating princess who could rival the goddess Freyja herself." He bites my jaw.

Heat spreads over my skin, and I bite my lip to stifle a moan, unwilling to give him the satisfaction of knowing that I love it when he calls me that. I used to hate it, but oh how things have changed.

"What I wouldn't give to ravish you right now," he says, fingers tangled in my hair.

"Why won't you? Too afraid my brother may come through the door at any moment."

He pulls away from me completely and lies flat on his back. "Don't ever mention Espen when we are being amorous."

"Did I dampen your spirits, Agnarr?" I roll on top of him. "Let's see if I can ignite them again."

I press my open lips to his, and his tongue instantly connects with mine. His arms curl around me and a mixture of pleasure and pain rolls through me. I had almost forgotten about my fall, but my skin has not. That means I need Agnarr to remind me just how pleasurable things can be. He effortlessly moves us into a sitting position. His mouth finds my neck as his hands trace the outline of my body, pulling off my tunic. I can feel myself getting lost in him when he stops.

His eyes are frozen on my torso. Glancing down, I see the entire right side is a horrifying shade of perse. I wrap my arms around myself and look away.

"Please stop looking at me." I reach for my tunic. He gently grabs my wrist, forcing my eyes back to him.

"It breaks me to see you like this. It is no wonder your mother and Espen were so worried."

"It's just a bruise." I pull my tunic back over my head and climb off him.

"Brynja, have I not proven already how much I desire you?"

Glancing over my shoulder, I can see the frustration in the hard lines of his face.

"I have wanted you for far longer than I care to admit, I just... don't want to hurt you. I have had bruises such as yours. I know how tender they are."

I want so desperately to be mad at him, but I cannot. His concern is real, as much as I want to dismiss it. Before I can respond, Thyra enters the room from the servants' door.

"Good morning, Your Royal Highness. Ma..."

She stops mid-sentence, eyes locked on Agnarr, who is still in my bed and shirtless. A smile pulls at the corner of Agnarr's lips. He waves at her. It takes her a moment, but she waves back before turning her attention to me. She is fighting with everything in her not to squeal.

"Apologies, ma'am." She bows. "May I bring you and your guest some breakfast?"

"That would be delightful, thank you, Thyra. Please be sure to bring enough coffee for all of us."

"Yes, ma'am." She smiles, unable to contain her excitement completely before disappearing out the door.

"I thought Espen to be a liar when he told me your friend was beautiful. I would have to agree. She is quite pleasing. Not as pleasing as you, of course. I always thought he was talking about that twin girl. What's her name?"

"Astrid."

"Yes, that's the one."

My heart soars at the thought that once I am better, I can see both her and Aksel without any concerns since my father is gone. How have I not thought about this until now? Perhaps we can even meet at the beach today. That does not require much, and the sun surely would be good for me. When Thyra returns, I will have her send word.

"What is on your mind, princess?" Agnarr asks, bringing my focus back to the room.

"The beach. I want to go to the beach."

AN HOUR LATER, my feet are in the sand and Astrid is sitting by my side. The ocean is violent, but the sun is warm and winsome. Aksel has taken it upon himself to entertain Agnarr. They have interacted many times but never without Espen. I'm truly thankful for his kindness.

"Are you going to tell me what happened to your face, or are we just going to pretend it's not there?"

"I had a run-in with some trees."

She burst out laughing. "Seriously Bryn. What happened?"

"I wish it were a joke, but it's not. I was training in the forest. I fell and almost tumbled to my death in a giant chasm."

"The Slaughter Hollow."

Intense horror pours into my veins. The chasm I almost tumbled into was the same place my father has sent far too many to their deaths. It has been rumored the look my father gets on his face before pushing someone off the edge rivals Hel's, the ruler of Niflheim. It does not surprise me. He finds pleasure in others' fear. I did not, however, realize how close Slaughter Hollow was to the palace.

"That does not make me feel any better, Astrid."

She takes my hands and holds them tightly between hers. "Do not think about it any longer. You survived. The gods smiled down upon you. You must move on."

I attempt to remove my hands from hers, but her grip is firm yet somehow soft. Our eyes meet and there is a lethal calmness in them.

"I wish you would see the strength in you that I do."

Her declaration is simple, but the truth behind her words rocks me to my core.

"I desire the same. You have such... fortitude."

She brings both our hands to her forehead briefly before planting a small kiss on them.

"You, sweet Bryn, can have anything you desire. You just have to trust yourself."

Mormor Thorsson always told me how powerful words can be. It's not that I never believed her, I just didn't *feel* it before. I feel Astrid's words flowing through me with every pump of my heart.

"Thank you, Astrid. Your words have brought me great comfort."

"Fabulous. Now come. Let's walk. I need to hear all about your newfound connection with Agnarr."

"How di—"

"He has looked over here no less than ten times. So don't bore me with your excuses and just provide the tantalizing details."

I can't stop the giggle in my chest, and I don't want to. It feels good to laugh. So, we giggle together and walk down the beach, sharing sultry stories.

By the time we make it back to the palace, the sun has set, and I have added a sunburn to my skin ailments. It was worth it as I got to spend my day with my friends, completely at ease. I can't remember the last time that was possible. I have lived under the shadow of my father for so long. I hoped to find my mother and brother upon our return, but the palace is hauntingly quiet.

When we enter the kitchen, there is only the chef and a large man in the corner. He has a plate of food in front of him but has not touched any of it. As I get closer, I recognize Orn, and if he is here, so are my mother and brother!

"Orn! It is so good to see you. Where are Mother and Espen?" Upon closer inspection, I see he is hurt. Blood covers his hands and is splattered all over his face. "You are hurt! Let me fetch th—"

"Please sit."

His words are so quiet I almost don't hear them, but I do as requested.

"I'm so sorry, Brynja." His tear-filled eyes meet mine. I reach for his hand and hold it firmly in mine. Before I can speak, he continues. "I tried to stop them, but I was outnumbered."

Fear flails in my veins. "Tried to stop who?"

"The king and his army, but I was useless. I am ashamed to call myself a guard of the royal family."

"Orn, you are not making any sense. What of the king?"

He uncurls my fingers and places something into my palm. I know what it is and what it means without seeing it.

I drop to my knees as a swell of pain shatters my last shreds of control. A raw scream of despair and disbelief wail from my lips. Agnarr and Astrid are at once by my side, but I push them away. I don't want love or any sort of touch. I want to light the world on fire.

"Orn, what is the meaning of this? What did you tell her?" Agnarr yells over my screams.

"I didn't need to tell her. She knows."

"Knows what? Stop your cryptic troll talk and tell us at once!"

"The queen and the prince are dead by orders of the king. Though he will deny it."

The words turn me into a fist of fury. I throw and break everything I can touch. Agnarr, Astrid, and even Aksel try to contain me, but there is nothing that can stop me. I take my wave of destruction to my room, demolishing every inch and everything my father ever gave me. Not even my clothes survive the massacre. They hang off me like drapes barely covering my body. I don't want anything that might have ever been near the king touching me. I raise a drawer over my head and charge at the mirror when I notice my reflection.

All my bruises are gone and the wound on my leg is nonexistent.

CHAPTER 7

The drawer plummets from my hands and splinters into pieces. How is this possible? Just a few hours ago, I was covered in bruises. I inhale a long breath, expecting the pain to at least remain, but nothing. I feel as strong as ever. Peering at my ankle, the scar from when I fell out of a boat as a child is still there. Whatever... happened only applied to my current injuries. Did the Goddess of Healing, Eir, visit me while I slept?

As I look over myself once more, my eyes land on my neck. At least in my tornado of rage, I had the sense to put it on me.

Espen's necklace.

Truthfully, I have no clue where he got it, but he never removed it. Ever. Made of braided leather, a wooden pendant hangs in the center. The pendant is dark at the top, but as it comes to a point, it goes from ocean blue to dazzling green. It appears just as the night sky during aurora borealis. Beautiful yet masculine, just like Espen. Now it is all I have left of him, and I will never remove it. I wrap my hand around the pendant, hoping it will connect me with him, but nothing.

Fury and heartbreak push themselves back to the surface, but now I want answers. I want to know why this happened. I replace my tattered clothes with new and tuck Espen's necklace safely underneath my tunic next to my skin.

In the kitchen, everyone is focused on cleaning up the mess I made. Part of me feels regret, yet at the same time, I want to burn the whole place to the ground.

"Tell me what happened, Orn."

Everyone stops and looks at me.

"Princess, wh—"

"I was not addressing you, Agnarr. Please, Orn. Tell me what happened."

Orn sets down whatever is in his hand and turns the table and chairs I had flipped back upright. He sits in one chair and motions for me to sit in the other. The last thing I want to do is sit, but Orn is being kind. Once seated, he begins.

"We were on the road returning from Thora. The queen, the prince , the lach, myself, and three other guards. They attacked out of nowhere, coming from every side. There was no escape. I killed as many as I could protecting your moth... the queen. She put up a strong fight herself, refusing to give up."

"What of Espen? He is... was superior with a sword. How did he not defeat them?" Using the past tense to describe my brother is like a knife in my heart.

"He tried, Brynja. There were just too many and they

were prepared. They lit the carriage on fire with the lach inside. I can still hear him screaming."

Acid burns the back of my throat as the scene plays out in my head. Such a cruel ending for his own blood.

"Why? Why did this happen? I don't understand. He made his dislike of us known but to kill…"

Orn curls his large hand around mine. "You were a part of the plan. There was quite a stir among the soldiers when they realized you were not present, but it is why they spared me."

I didn't think this moment could get worse, but it had. The king had planned to kill off his entire family but due to my… foolishness I managed to avoid it. How did he even get word they had gone to Thora? Someone in the palace undoubtedly can't be trusted.

"You must leave, Brynja," Orn says, his hand tightening around mine.

"Leave? And go where?" I have no place to go. I refuse to go to Thora and put anyone else in danger.

"It doesn't matter but you can't stay here. He will come for you."

"Why, Orn? Why?"

"To send a message to Sigvard. He has killed a large portion of the king's army, including the king's brother. By killing you, your father shows that Thoracian blood will not be tolerated. Not even his own family. He will not stop until Sigvard and the rebellion are dead."

I resist the urge to start destroying everything again. All of this because of one man. I try to focus on anything else, but Agnarr left the room in a fit of rage, and Astrid and Aksel were not far behind him. Once Orn is gone as well, I will have to face it all.

The death of my mother.

My brother.

Myself.

I can't let Orn die too.

"I can't do anything until I know you will be safe."

Orn lets out a slow laugh. "Do not worry about me, sweet Brynja. If it is my time, I am ready. I have had a good life. You have much left to do."

"I have nothing, Orn." I look away from him, attempting to hold back the waterfall of tears.

Unexpectedly, Orn picks me up and pulls me into his lap. He holds me tightly while running his hand over my hair. There is no stopping the tears now.

"I know it feels that way, but this is far from the end," he says, his voice soft.

"How do you know that?" I mumble against his chest.

"Because I believe you were spared for a reason. Now you need to find out what that reason is."

I press myself deeper into his grasp, hoping, wishing I can just vanish from the world. "How will I ever know? It is not like I can ask someone."

"Perhaps not, but that is not out of the realm of possibilities. Seers do exist, my lady."

I have only ever spoken to a seer once. She was a dear friend of Mormor Thorsson, but her name escapes my memory. Maybe I could make a short trip to Thora to see if she still resides there? The true question is, where will I go after? Orn is right. I cannot stay here. I would forever be looking over my shoulder.

"Will you come with me?" I sit up in his lap so I may gaze into his face. The fear of leaving is great but far greater is leaving alone.

"I would be honored, Princess, but I must stay to

protect those who remain. I am one of the few surviving guards."

"But without anyone here, why would any of you stay? We should all leave."

"Death awaits us either way. The king will hunt us down and kill us if we leave or we can stand together and die among friends and familiarity."

I wrap my arms around him and hug him tightly. Orn has been with me for as long as I can remember, and as much as I want to stay and be with him until the end, I know I can't. I need to avenge my mother and brother. Pulling myself out of his lap I smooth out my clothes and do my best to stand confidently in front of him.

"Will you do me a favor, Orn?"

"Anything, Princess," he says shifting his weight, so he is leaning toward me.

"Will you make sure they receive a proper ceremony? No one will expect me to leave prior and as much as it pains me to leave before... I know I must."

"I would be honored. The smoke shall reach as high as the heavens."

"And be sure Espen has his sword. He cannot go to Valhalla without one.

"It is already with him, and it is where it shall remain."

I nod as the reality of what I must do takes hold. In a matter of moments, I have lost everything and everyone I know. I turn to leave but my feet are unable to move, knowing that once I leave there is no turning back. My hand finds Espen's necklace again.

"Please be with me, brother," I whisper, squeezing the pendant tighter. My eyes fill with tears again. I never imagined I would be facing this world without him, let alone a war. It's then I grasp I have been lacking in my appreciation for Orn. I shake away my emotions the best I can and turn back to him.

"Thank you, Orn. His necklace has already brought me such comfort."

"It is the least I could do, Princess. Now go, before I start to shed tears. I can't have you remembering me as a blubbering old blob."

"You could never be any of those things!" I dash into his arms for one final hug. We do not speak or move for several moments before I finally retreat to what is left of my bedroom.

I look around the disheveled room, trying to decide what to take with me. Whatever I bring I will have to carry. What's more is I don't have anything to put my things in. My brother would have something, but that would require venturing into his room and I'm not sure my heart can handle it. I sit on the floor in the middle of the chaos and take several deep breaths. As much as I want to hide in the shadows and mourn, I don't have the time. I must swallow my feelings and move on.

The door to Espen's bedroom creaks as I open it. There is a chill in the air, but his smell still lingers. The room is frozen in time, waiting for his return. A moment that will never occur.

The room is simple. Not much about except for a few books on the nightstand. I run my fingers along the edge of the bed frame before settling onto the mattress. I'm taken back to that morning not long ago when Espen woke me from my nightmare. What I wouldn't give to go back there.

The first book is titled *Heavenly Bodies*. Of course, my brother would be interested in the female form, but when I open the pages, I find it has nothing to do with that at all. It is rather a detailed publication about the world above our heads. The stars. The moon. The planets. Espen has written numbers in the ledger, but I have no idea what they mean. Regardless, the find makes me smile.

The second book is ironically titled *Sword War*. The book has been read so much the title is partially worn off and the edges frayed. Inside, the notes Espen has left cover almost every page. He has also underlined countless paragraphs. I pull down the covers of his bed and curl up underneath them. I know I shouldn't, but I want to spend but a moment lost in his pastime. In his... memory.

―

"Your Royal Highness. Ma'am. You must wake up!"

My eyes snap open to someone sitting beside me. I cannot make out who it is in the darkness, and the fogginess of sleep has cloaked whose voice stirred me from slumber.

"Ma'am, you must get up. There is news the king is coming to mourn."

This revives me immediately. If the king is on his way, I no longer have a moment to waste. I remove myself from the covers as a candle is lit, and I am able to see Thyra. Yet another friend I will have to leave behind.

"Thank you for rousing me." I smile.

"Of course, ma'am. It is my duty. I have also found this bag in Espen's closet. Perhaps you can use it on your travels."

How she always knows exactly what I need will never cease to amaze me. I take the bag and toss the two books from Espen's nightstand inside. Additionally, I take Espen's favorite tunic from his drawer before returning to my room. I obtain my training gear from my room, a fur for when the colder months come, and several bags of coin. I remove my current attire and as I put on each piece, it feels different. Like I am truly preparing for war, which means I have one place I must go before I leave.

"I will see Agnarr before departing for Thora," I say to Thyra's reflection in the mirror.

"I figured as much, ma'am. Orn has prepared a horse. It is waiting on the hidden path to Vildmark."

"How will I survive without you both?" I face her.

She smiles fully while clasping her hands around my shoulders. "You are more than capable, ma'am. I know it. You know it."

We hug each other tightly. Thyra has always given the best hugs. Just the right amount of pressure and warmth. I will miss her beyond measure.

"Take care of yourself, my dear friend." I squeeze her slightly tighter.

"And you as well, Brynja. I have a feeling our paths will cross again."

We pull away from the hug but continue holding hands.

"I will hold tight to that idea." I go to leave, but she holds tight to one of my hands.

"Before you leave, I have one more thing for you."

Curious, I watch as she strides across the room and pulls a box out from under my bed. A smart place to hide it as I would never look there. She hands me the box and steps back to watch me open it. Inside is a teal cross-shouldered cloak. It is simple yet somehow stunningly beautiful.

"Come, ma'am. Let me help you. One last time."

We exchange smiles, and I turn back to the mirror. She slides the cloak over my head. It veils across my shoulders and pools comfortably around my body. Thyra tucks my braid behind me before pulling the hood over my head.

"Now you are ready. Go quickly!"

Her words shoot through me like a star cascading across the night sky, and my feet are moving before my heart can stop me.

I had hoped to see Orn waiting by the horse but no such luck. I must carry on. Getting to Agnarr's is much faster by horse. I am there before I can put together everything I want to say to him, but whatever I can manage will have to do.

He answers the door, and I paste on a small smile. Agnarr, on the other hand, appears vexed.

"What do you want? I figured you would be long gone by now," he says, his body shielding the door.

"I don't want to leave without you, but we must go. The king is coming."

He laughs a deep, scornful laugh, causing shame to blossom in my belly.

"You truly think I would go anywhere with you? Stop wasting both our time and be gone."

Confusion tumbles through me, but I do my best to keep the emotion off my face. Agnarr has always been difficult to understand, but this complete change in sentiment toward me is appalling. He must be joking.

"Agnarr, now is not the time. Come. Grab your stuff and let us leave this place."

"I would rather die than go anywhere with *you*."

The word "you" is deeply laced with distaste and his eyes, which had previously been filled with desire, now blaze with disgust.

"Agna—"

"Do NOT speak my name. I never again want to hear my name on your lips."

"But... why?"

His scornful laugh makes another ghastly appearance.

"You truly are oblivious sometimes, Princess. You want to know why I hate you? Why I can't stand the sight of you?"

I nod even though I don't want the answer.

"It is because you purposely caused a fight between me and my best friend and now, HE IS DEAD! His last memory of me is breaking a promise and now... now I can never make it up to him."

I didn't think my heart could break any further but whatever pieces remained are gone. A cold chill of emptiness runs through my veins as I force myself to look at Agnarr.

"That may be true, but you weren't the only one he was mad at, and I lost him too. Along with my mother and everything I have ever known. You want me gone, Agnarr, you shall have your wish."

I turn on my heels and leave. There is no need for any additional words to be spoken. Being unwanted is a feeling I am all too familiar with. It is time for me to face this world on my own. I will stop in Thora and speak to the seer. Afterward, I will find a new home in the wilderness. There is no need for humankind anymore. The name is misleading. Let them all kill each other, I will find my happiness elsewhere.

I'm prepared to mount my horse when I hear a rustling in the trees. Previously I would have been scared and just rode off, but I no longer care.

"Who is there? Make yourself known."

"It's just me, ma'am. I couldn't bear the thought of our friendship ending so abruptly." Thyra appears from the edge of the forest.

The sight of her slightly warms my cold blood.

"As much as I would love for you to come with it, it is not safe."

"Neither is staying here, ma'am."

"Please stop calling me ma'am. The days of you having to serve me are gone."

"So, we are just friends?" She stands directly in front of me. I nod once. "Then if we are friends, let me come with you."

Her gesture is so kind I decide to be brutally honest with her. "I cannot handle losing another person I love, Thyra. If we end up in a battle I don't know if I would be able to protect you."

"It is a good thing I am well-versed in the sword then." She smiles. I try to smile back but any emotion other than despair is difficult. I want to say yes because I don't want to be alone, but it also feels incredibly selfish even with her request. I go to speak, but she beats me to it.

"Please, Brynja."

My soul is still screaming at me to say no, but instead I nod, and we ride off together to Thora.

CHAPTER 8

Thankfully, Thora looks just as I remember it. I had feared the king's army had destroyed it considering Sigvard hails from here and what he did to his own family, but currently Thora remains untouched. Mormor Thorsson passed long ago, but her youngest sister, my Great-aunt Runy, has never left Thora. Her home is located on the far side of town, and as we ride past all the townspeople, I feel as if every eye is on me. I have never felt so exposed. I decide to take a risk and pull down my hood, allowing everyone to see me. This will go one of two ways. Acceptance or death.

"Good morning, Thora. Please don't be afraid. It is only I, Brynja, and I come to you unarmed."

I hold my breath, waiting for the arrow in my back, when a young lady approaches and bows.

"Your Royal Highness, it is so good to see you. What brings you to Thora?"

I dismount and stand before her proudly. Clearly, word of what happened has not made it this far yet. I take her hands in mine and gently guide her out of her bow.

"I come for supplies and to speak to my great-aunt. Please tell me she is still amongst you."

"She is, ma'am. What supplies do you need? I would be happy to fetch them for you."

"What is your name?" I make eye contact with her.

"Asta, ma'am."

"It is nice to meet you, Asta. Please call me Brynja. Would you do me the favor of gathering everyone? I wish to speak to them all."

"Of course, ma... Brynja."

I nod my thanks and walk the horse the rest of the way to Runy's home. Thyra remains comfortably on its back, taking in the town. I can tell she is enjoying the freedom and me spoiling her but refuses to acknowledge it out loud. This makes me smile. She deserves to feel free.

I stand outside Runy's door, playing over and over in my head how unpleasant this is going to be. I also try to remember the last time I saw her. The fact that I can't clearly remember indicates it has been far too long. Just as I have mustered up the courage to knock, the door swings open.

"Are you here to see me or just my door?" she asks, her sapphire eyes twinkling. Great-aunt Runy is advanced in her years, but her beauty has not faded. All I can manage to do is give her a thin smile. She wraps her arms around me. The warmth of her embrace instantly has me missing my mother, and I have to fight to keep composure.

"Why do I have this feeling you are not here just for a visit?" Her words are soft and musical.

"Because I am not."

"Then you best come in. I have a fresh pot of stew."

Runy sets a steaming bowl in front of me and even though it has been days since I have eaten, I do not feel hungry. The only feelings I have slide between anguish and numbness. She watches. waiting to see what I do. Thyra sits beside me, slowly slurping the stew after exchanging pleasantries with Runy.

"This... news must be horrid. Your lack of appetite and eye contact is beyond disconcerting."

I nod, unsure if I have the strength to say the words, but I will have to find them. I had Asta gather the townspeople, but I can't stand before them mute. I clear my throat and say a silent prayer to the god Thor to share even the slightest bit of his strength with me.

"My mother and brother have gone to Valhalla." Runy remains still with her eyes on me. "It was my fath... the king who ordered it."

"But they were just here. When did this happen?" She somehow remains tranquil.

"On their way back from Thora, they were attacked."

"And what of the lach? Did he survive?" I shake my head. "So, they killed them all...No mercy. And if the lach never arrived, how are you healed? According to Espen, you were in grim condition."

Hearing Espen's name is like a cold hand tightening around my throat. What I wouldn't give to speak with him again.

"I wish I had an answer, Aunt Runy, but I do not know how I healed. One morning I awoke, and all my injuries were... gone." I tried to stop there, but the question rolls off my lips. "What else did Espen say?"

She sits on the other side of me and wraps an arm tightly around my shoulders. "He was terrified, Brynja.

Absolutely beside himself you would die. That he would not be able to tell you how much you mean to him."

The tears pour down my face before I can stop them. My brother and I shared the same fear.

"We had a fight... and I never got to..." My words are garbled by the tears. Aunt Runy kneels in front of me.

"Trust me when I say he knew without a doubt that you loved him. The relationship you two had was unlike anything I have ever witnessed. Since you were children, the two of you were bonded. That bond could not be shattered by a mere disagreement."

"They were remarkable, weren't they?" Thyra's words surprise me. She has not spoken since the forest outside of Agnarr's house. She smiles, but her gaze is still on her stew. "I have not witnessed such sibling love either."

"Agreed and I am so, so sorry you have not only lost him but your wonderful mother. I can't imagine the pain you are in. Why don't you stay with me for a while? It would be my honor to have you."

Her simple gesture is enough to halt my tears. I have dreamed of a home where I was wanted. Yes, my mother wanted me, but it was not enough to make the palace feel welcoming. The burden was far too large for her to overcome. I meet my eyes with hers.

"I would love to stay with you, but I refuse to put you at risk. The king killed his wife and his heir. I can't fathom what he might do if he finds out I am here."

A depth of sadness sinks into the lines of her face, but she nods in understanding. Now that I have told Aunt Runy, I must tell the rest of the town. They deserve to know about their queen and their prince. It will also remove the element of surprise should the king decide to come here.

Asta did as requested. All the townspeople are gathered

and waiting for me. Their faces are a mix of pride and panic. I do not blame them. I stand on a rock to give myself some height and the ability to see each and every face.

"Sweet people of Thora. It pains me to tell you..." I swallow hard, trying to moisten my dry mouth and throat. "Queen Anitra and Prince Espen are dead."

Waves of surprise roll over the crowd as they mumble to each other.

"That is not all. The king ordered it."

The mumbling grows to a vicious roar with the new information as their surprise transforms into anger.

"He will, of course, deny this, but I have heard it from the one person who survived the attack. Unfortunately, your lach, I apologize for not knowing his name, has also been killed." Before the crowd can turn into a violent pack, I continue. "Due to the danger my presence imposes, I will be leaving shortly. I only came to inform my family and all of you and to purchase some supplies. I require a sword. Who here can provide me with one?"

"Me as well!" Thyra shouts from behind me. That reminds me to question her later when and how she became well-versed with a sword.

"It would be my honor, Your Royal Highness." I search the crowd for where the voice came from but am unable to pinpoint the source.

"Please come forward and make yourself known."

A man with shoulders that appear to be sculpted from boulders steps forward. "It would give me great pleasure to make a sword for you, ma'am."

"Call me Brynja. As far as I am concerned, I am no longer royal. I am just... a person."

"I do not agree but as you wish. Come with me."

I follow the man around the square to a large brick

building. Inside, it is hot as Niflheim and several men are pounding furiously at cherry red steel. I imagine this as a lower version of how Mjölnir was created for Thor.

"How much do you weigh?" he asks.

"Excuse me?" What does my weight have to do with anything?

"It helps me to determine how much your sword should weigh. That and your hands." He reaches out but waits for my permission. I nod, and he takes my hand, flipping it over so my palm is up. His rough hand trails over mine up to my elbow and back again. I feel a strange heat in the wake of his touch but blame it on the condition of the room. "You are very familiar with a sword, but it seems the one you were using was far too long."

"How can you possibly know that?" Our eyes find each other. His are the color of the fires roaring behind him.

"By your calluses. See how you have some here on the edge of your thumb and the top of your forefinger? That tells me you were fighting against it falling out of your hands."

"That is amazing." I am truly impressed by his ability to gain such information from my calluses. He closes my palm and places his hand over it.

"I think I have just the blade for you. Let me put some finishing touches on it."

"Thank you..." I do not like not knowing the name of the person I am addressing.

"Booth. My name is Booth, Princess."

That fact that he calls me "Princess" hits my emotions in numerous ways. One is a stinging reminder of Agnarr.

"Thank you, Booth. May I send my friend in here? She will need a sword as well."

"I will make sure she has something sufficient for her

needs. Now you must excuse me. I have work to do." He winks and strolls off.

I had additional questions, the main one being how long it takes to create a sword. I honestly have no clue and do not want to stay here any longer than necessary, but I can't leave her without one either. I will have to be patient. Patient and watchful.

That night I lie in bed wide awake watching the starry sky. I forgot how peaceful and alluring the sky is when a giant palace isn't obscuring it. I can watch each star twinkling individually, dazzling me with its celestial dance. Which reminds me of the book I found on Espen's nightstand. I pull the book from my bag under the bed and begin to read.

Seeing the pages laced with Espen's scribbles makes me feel closer to him, and my body relaxes some for the first time since I received the news. Yes, I have his necklace, and it does bring me great comfort but his familiar script evokes a different level of solace.

"I miss him too, you know," Thyra says. She faces me on her bed, her long hair encircling her face. I don't believe I have ever seen her with her hair down.

"What do you miss most about him?" I am desperate to hear a good story.

"I will tell you, but you must promise not to get upset."

Upset? What in the gods is she talking about? "Why would I get upset, Thyra?"

She presses up onto her elbow and tucks her hair behind her ear. "Because I knew your brother in a very... intimate way."

"You and Espen? Truly? For how long? Is that how you know how to wield a sword? I should have known!" I throw my arms down on the bed.

Thyra looks at me, speechless. I think she was expecting me to be shocked, but if I am being honest, I should have put it together long ago. His kind words to her. The winks. Espen is a gentleman, but there are subtle things he saves for people he likes. Winks are one of them.

"Wait? You aren't upset?"

"No, Thyra. How could I be? My brother and only friend found love together. Truth be told, I find it *worthy of song*. I just wish you both would have trusted me enough to tell me."

"It wasn't because of trust, Brynja. We wanted something that was just for us."

I nod, understanding how important that is. "I don't mean to sound selfish, but did you two ever discuss... Agnarr and me?"

"I wish I could say we had, but we did not meet after that occurred."

"Where did you meet?"

"Do you know that little shed on the far edge of the property? The one that looks like it could collapse at any moment?"

"Yes! You did not meet there. That place has to be riddled with snakes and bugs."

"I thought the same, but Espen must have cleaned it up. At least on the inside. There were furs on the floor. Candles."

"So, my brother was a romantic."

"Very much so."

Tears stream down my face. I am so tired of crying, but I can't stop it. I can only hope I will run out soon. Thyra slides into bed next to me and wraps her arms around me.

"I can't imagine what you are feeling, but I can promise

that you will never be alone as long as I have air in my lungs."

I choke on a mixture of my tears and a laugh. Not because I don't believe her, but because I do. I don't know how in the chaos that is my life the gods managed to send me Thyra.

"You should wear your hair down more. You look beautiful."

This makes her chuckle a little as well. "Thankfully, I can now that we no longer live under the king's thumb."

We snuggle in closer together and I read aloud from Espen's book, temporarily forgetting everything we still face. In this moment, the only thing that matters is we have each other.

When I awake, Thyra is gone and light streams in through the window. That is the first night I have gotten good sleep in ages. It is also the first time I feel the pain of hunger.

Downstairs, I find Aunt Runy stirring a pot and Thyra by the window drinking what I can only assume is coffee, her favorite thing.

"Good morning," I say happily.

"You look much better today. Would you like some eggs or coffee?"

"Both please, Aunt Runy."

A wide smile spreads across her face as she spoons out some eggs and pours me a fresh cup of coffee.

"Booth was already here today. Your swords are ready." Aunt Runy watches me finish my eggs and quickly refills my plate.

"That seems quick. Did he work all night?"

"I believe he did."

"I didn't think that was a process that could be rushed. I

will go to him as soon as I am finished." It's at that moment I realize I have no idea what the proper payment would be for such work. "Aunt Runy, may I ask you a question?"

"Of course, dear."

"I want to ensure I give Booth his worth. I do not wish to insult him. What would be a proper payment?"

"You have always been so thoughtful, Brynja." She moves closer and closes a hand around mine. "Please know what I say next is not meant as an insult, merely to inform you."

I nod, wanting to understand as much as I can of the world I have been kept from.

"Comfort is our main concern in Thora. We require very little and are truly happy that way. That being said, a significant amount of coin is not something we see very often, if ever."

Although I acknowledge what Aunt Runy is telling me, it does not truly answer the question. Enjoying the simple things is wonderful, but that does not negate the fact that Booth should be paid properly for his services.

"Simple life or not, I wish to pay Booth what he has earned."

"I wish I could answer you, but I am truthfully not sure."

"Ten ounces of silver, ma'am."

Thyra's voice surprises me. She had been quietly sipping her coffee in the corner, but her sudden inclusion in the conversation has me looking at her with wide eyes.

"How on earth do you know that, Thyra?"

"Espen." She smiles gently. "The king put him in charge of getting new swords for the army. Out of curiosity, I asked him how much all those new swords would cost. It was four hundred ounces of silver for fifty swords. That is eight ounces a piece. Knowing the king and his miserly ways, I added two additional ounces, figuring that would be fair."

I turn back to Aunt Runy. "What do you think? Does ten ounces of silver per sword sound fair?"

"It would be life changing."

A satisfied grin pulls at my lips, and I feel some hope for the first time in days. I wash the remaining eggs down with coffee and go to see Booth.

When I arrive, the building is sweltering hot, and half a dozen men are working furiously. Most of them are shirtless and covered in a layer of dirt and sweat. Although my desire has recently been quenched, it does not mean such a sight will go unnoticed. The smell alone could bring even the strongest woman to their knees.

Some of their eyes fall on me. A scent of a woman in their ranks is something they would be hard-pressed to ignore as well. I move to address one of them when a hand falls on my shoulder.

"Are you here to distract my men or pick up your swords?" Booth asks, a small smirk forming on his lips. I thought he was handsome before, but his smile only intensifies the thought.

"Perhaps both," I say, feeling playful.

"Well, then. How about I show you the swords and you distract them at lunch when they are not being paid?"

"Deal."

I follow him through a labyrinth of rooms until we stop in what appears to be an armory of sorts. The room is not only filled with swords, but every weapon forged from steel one could imagine.

"I picked out something unique for your handle. It was given to me years ago, and I never knew what to do with it until now." He walks over to a table covered with a cloth, and elation flows through me. "Come. You do the honors."

I stand beside him, holding my breath as the pain of Espen's absence washes over me. Grief is peculiar like that. One moment you are fine and the next it hits you like a tidal wave. I close my eyes, wishing him back into existence, when I feel a gentle flurry of air around my hand.

"Is that you?" I squeeze my eyes closed even tighter.

"Princess, are you alright?"

I try to ignore Booth's words, but that is all it took for me to lose hold of... whatever that was. I open my eyes and force myself to focus on Booth.

"Yes. Apologies, I was just lost in thought."

He doesn't look convinced but nods anyway, so I peel back the cloth. Underneath are two utterly striking swords. One has an onyx handle and looks absolutely terrifying on its own accord. I can't imagine the fear it will invoke once bloody on the battlefield. The other has a white handle.

I'm reminded of my previous visions. Of the vibrating white sword with the crimson tip. This sword is not the same, but it is astonishingly similar. I reach out to pick it up and the moment my fingertips touch the hilt, I am shifted in time.

I'm in the forest, and this time, I'm not only surrounded by trees but by men. I seem to be alone, and they are closing in. The part of me that I am familiar with is panicked, but the part of me that these visions bring out is... furious. I don't have time to consider how I feel or where I am when I begin to tear through each and every one of them with my blade. Scarlet blood coats the trees and my cheeks, but nothing can stop me. Just as my sword is about to make another strike, the world crumbles around me.

A gasp unfurls from my lips, and when I open my eyes, I

am bent over the table with the two swords. Booth is directly beside me, a hand on my lower back.

"Princess, are you okay?"

I close my eyes and shake the remaining cobwebs from my mind. I wish I could steady my mind. Or these visions. Or at least understand how and why they come. Agnarr is the only constant I have been able to pinpoint.

"Yes, I'm fine, Booth. I just... lost my breath for a moment."

I push myself up and face him, not realizing just how close we are. My eyes are directly in line with his glistening neck, and he smells of metal mixed with sweet brown sugar. I have the urge to lick his defined edges to see which one he tastes like more. Now I truly was losing my breath.

"It's selenite," he says, clearing his throat and reaching for the sword. Perhaps I am not the only one fighting off urges. He places the sword on one finger roughly three inches from the hilt. "It's also perfectly balanced."

I would swear he was performing a magic trick if I didn't know any better. He hands me the sword and then backs away, giving me space to try it. Under normal circumstances, I would feel reserved but just having this sword in my hand makes me feel... powerful.

I slice the blade side to side and even with its weight, it feels light. Espen always told me the sword should feel like an extension of my body. I thought I had grasped that concept but hadn't truly until this moment. This sword was made for me, and I can feel it in every aspect, from the hilt to the tip.

"I didn't think the sword could be any more perfect but, you are a natural."

I laugh softly. "I wish. Years of practice."

"Even with years of practice, some will never move like

you do." He takes the sword back from me and runs a cloth over the sharp edge. "Come. I have a few more things for you." He grabs the other sword and walks to another room.

This room is filled with every kind of accessory one could imagine. Leather belts, shields, scabbards, jackets, and more. I pick up a small leather scabbard and inside is a curved blade with a curved handle just barely the length of my palm.

"That is a buffalo horn knuckle hatchet. Take it. Stick it in your boot. It's a good backup defense if you find yourself in a pickle."

"Oh no, I can't take this, Booth."

"You can and you will."

Not wishing to argue or insult the man, I stick the small hatchet into my boot as instructed.

"You and Thyra will also need these," he says, pulling a sheet off a large table to expose a litany of gear. I am left speechless. I merely came to the man for a sword, yet he has gone out of this way to ensure we are protected.

"This is beyond anything I could have imagined. Thank you."

"We certainly can't have the princess and her partner in crime going out unprepared. Now let me make sure everything fits properly."

He starts by wrapping a pair of leather greaves around my legs. They run from my ankle to just below my knee, offering additional protection. They do not look like much, but they can withstand blows from a blade that may otherwise prove detrimental. Next, he suits me with a scabbard. It goes around my waist like a belt, then up across my chest and around my back. On the back side is a place for my sword so I don't have to carry it. He puts the sword inside and I expect it to be heavy, but the weight is balanced across the scabbard.

"Now, reach back and remove your sword. Want to make sure we have it at the proper height."

I am unable to pull it out smoothly on the first attempt, but after a few adjustments, the sword pulls free from the scabbard like butter on bread. The last object Booth hands me is a set of beautiful steel bracers with a line of selenite through the center. Bracers are usually just leather wrapped around the wrists like I currently have and like the greaves he just equipped me with. These are designed as cuffs to go over the leather and provide additional protection. I place them on and squeeze so they are closed enough for comfort but not open enough to fall off. The shine from the metal and the twinkle of the selenite make them look more like a beautiful piece of jewelry than protection.

"They are stunning, Booth. Thank you."

"I had some selenite left. Figured I might as well put it to good use. I hope it gives you all the intuition you need in battle." A smile of pride softens his facial features.

Selenite is typically used to purify and cleanse spaces, but it is also believed to provide enhanced intuition and spiritual experience. Perhaps it will also keep me connected with my brother.

"I can't thank you enough. This has exceeded every expectation."

"It has been my pleasure, Princess," he says, bowing slightly.

I reach into my pocket and pull out one of the bags of silver. I remove thirty coins and place them into his hands, backing away before he can protest. The coins spill out onto the floor as he realizes how much I gave him.

"I cannot acc—"

"Yes, you can, and you will."

He smirks at having his own words used against him. He is also smart enough to know there is no arguing. He gathers the coins before putting them into his pockets. I attempt to pick up Thyra's gear, but he stops me.

"No. Please, send her here. I would like to make sure everything fits her."

"Of course. I will send her immediately."

Our eyes lock and I swear for a moment he is going to kiss me, but just as quickly as the moment came, Booth is gone.

CHAPTER 9

After nightfall, I walk the streets of the city, keeping watch and biding my time. Leave too early and we risk the possibility of running into others, but during the cover of night, in the wee hours, everyone is asleep, making it the best option. Thyra is currently sleeping, saving up energy for our journey. I am too worried to sleep. Worried and anxious. I'm also using it as an excuse to get used to everything I am now carrying. The last thing I need is to be encumbered.

As I make my way around the backside of the building where Booth works, I see him dividing up scraps. Or at least that is what it looks like he is doing.

"Do you ever stop working?" I stop in front of him, resting my hands on the belt of my new scabbard.

He smirks and tosses the last piece into the barrel. "Busy hands keep me out of trouble," he says, his smile widening as he takes in my appearance. "Being a warrior was meant for you."

I can't stop myself from spinning in a circle, giving him the full view. "Truly?"

He chuckles softly. "Abso-fucking-lutely."

The moonlight on his hardened features makes him even more attractive. Earlier in the day, he had been in long sleeves despite the heat, but he has since shed it. His arms are almost large enough to rival his shoulders and his chin has a dimple that softens him slightly. It's like the steel he works with. It's soft for a short period before it hardens into a beautiful piece of art.

I remember the first time I found a man attractive. I was fifteen. His family lived next to Mormor Thorsson. We never got along. In fact, we spent most of our youth torturing each other. He got caught in a trap I set and spent a good part of the afternoon upside down. I got catapulted into the muck on the far side of the lake. It all changed when I turned fifteen and I noticed his eyes. I had seen them thousands of times before, but it was like seeing them for the first time.

Eyes always grab my attention first. You can tell so much about a person by their eyes. They are the compass of a map. The key to unlocking all the answers. Secrets. Booth's blazing firestorm eyes are no exception. There is much more to this man aside from hard manual labor.

"If you never stop working, then when do you sleep?" I pull myself out of his gaze before I catch fire.

"I find time here and there." The handsome smile on his face reaches his eyes and bursts into a sensuous flame. Fuck.

"What else do you do to keep your hands busy when

you aren't making swords in one day?" I can't stop myself from asking or the sensual way it comes off my lips.

His gaze rakes boldly over my body.

"Princess Brynja, I don't want to be presumptuous, but ar—"

"What if I am?" If I let him be too much of a gentleman, this will halt before it even starts.

"You have a ten second head start."

Head start? What the Niflheim is he talking about? I thought we were on the same page but maybe not?

"One."

"Head start for what?"

"Two."

"Am I supposed to run!?"

"Three."

Brynja, you already lost three seconds, stop being a muttonhead and move your arse. I bound past him and inside the building. It is warm inside but not the sweltering hotbox it was when I first met Booth, who I can already hear behind me.

I dart toward a long hallway, weaving in and out of the different workstations and hoping I can confuse Booth even if just momentarily. I'm at the cusp of the next hallway when he catches my wrist.

When he spins me around, it happens fast and slow all at the same time. The loose pieces of my hair fly around me like the ends of a whip, our faces mere inches apart. My chest is heaving both from the run and the adrenaline. Booth is completely stoic. Like a lion who has just caught his prey. Trying to decide if he wants to toy with it or dive in for his meal.

He throws me over his shoulder with no effort and carries me to a workstation. He sets me down on the utility block. It is still warm from the day's work and all the metal he has bent to his will. The question is, can he do the same to me?

"I am not one of your projects," I tease him, smiling.

"Oh, indeed you are, Princess." He smirks as he strips my trousers and places a single kiss on my ankle. "A very rare... special project."

He drags his lips over my skin from my ankle up to the crest of my thigh. Using his breath, he encircles my cunt with a hot tornado of desire before dragging his lips down my opposite leg. I grip the block, hoping it can transfer some of its strength to me.

"Hold on tight, Princess. I plan to take my time with you." Each word sends a tingling sensation up my spine.

He hooks his thumbs into my panties, and I lift my arse so he can easily slide them off. Once removed, he makes a quick pass over my clit with his thumb. I jump at his touch, but he is already focused somewhere else.

"As sexy as you look in all this gear, it is not necessary for this adventure. It must be removed." His smile spreads across his face, lighting up his eyes again. If I was one of his projects, I would be nothing but molten metal.

One by one, he removes every article I have on my body and places it meticulously on the floor. I am completely bare and in between wanting to shield myself with my hands and owning it. Shifting my weight, I close my eyes and tell myself to relax, I started this.

"You might want to open your eyes." His smooth voice brings my focus back to him. He is standing in front of me just out of arm's reach, unbuttoning his trousers. I hold my breath as I watch him remove them in what feels like slow motion. What I wasn't anticipating was his lack of an undergarment.

When I was a teen, my mother and I used to go to the local market to see all the artists. There was every kind you could imagine. Painters, clay workers, sculptors. A woman who doubled as a prostitute made the most spectacular sculptures of the men she encountered. Booth would have been a perfect model for her. He is the epitome of strength. Magnetism. I am suddenly not feeling worthy of him. I attempt to rise from the block as panic sets in, but he holds up his hand.

"What is troubling you, Brynja?" The use of my name stops me. "If you have changed your mind, you merely need to voice that, and I will leave you be."

"It's... I don't... I'm not..." Words fumble out of my mouth as I try to vocalize my emotions.

"You are not what?" He moves closer. I can't stop myself from watching his girth swing side to side.

"Worthy." The single word comes from my lips before I can stop it. I'm not sure how I even formed a word. He is every delicious distraction I could ever formulate in my imagination in one man.

"How could you possibly think that? You are the most stunning woman I have ever laid eyes on."

He goes to circle around me, but I grab his wrist tightly. "Please don't."

He comes back in front of me, his eyes still burning with deep desire as they had when this first began. "You do not need to hide from me. What do you think you could be carrying that would send me for the hills?"

I bite my lip so hard the taste of iron floods my mouth. Sharing a night with a man is not new, clearly, but I have always managed to keep my secret, either by staying covered or just pure avoidance. This is not going to work with Booth unless I run, and I'm tired of running.

I let go of his wrist, close my eyes, and nod. The soft pads of his feet circle around me and I can already feel the tears encroaching on the corners of my eyes. His fingertips lightly brush where the top of my back where it meets my shoulders. An odd sensation of pain and pleasure rolls through me.

"Sweet Brynja, who did this to you?" he asks as a gentle finger traces down one of my scars.

"The king." My words are cold and short.

He stops immediately as the truth hits him. I expect him to cease entirely and walk away in disgust, both from my appearance and the actions of the king, but instead, I am met by the soft touch of his lips. It is so soft, so kind, that it takes me a few moments to truly appreciate what is happening.

"You should have never known such torture, especially at the hands of the king." His voice is quiet and tender as he resumes leaving kisses on the scars covering my back. Usually touching my scars can be quite painful, but his compassionate touch has the opposite effect. No one touches my scars except Thyra when she bathes me, and she knows exactly how to care for them. She has been doing it for years at this point.

Each touch of his finger, each soft kiss and brush of his breath, has my desire climbing. He presses his chest into me, and I relax into his form, letting my head fall to the side. His lips have not left my skin, and I wish I could hold on to this feeling forever.

"I thought I was going to take my time with you before, now I will not stop until every doubt in your heart is gone."

"Why are you being so kind? You don't know me, truly."

"I don't need to know you to know you are incredible," he says as his hand moves down my chest. "A beautiful woman." He continues lower, leaving goosebumps in the wake of his touch. "So sexy that you make me tremble with need."

He rests his large palm on my pelvis, gripping me mildly as he uses his pinky to play with my clit. I didn't think he could manage much with just his pinky, but he swirls and plays with the pristine combination of soft and firm. I relax deeper into his grip as a moan rolls off my tongue.

"That's it, Princess, succumb to me. Nothing else exists except you and me."

I look up at him, needing to see his eyes. They are burning as bright as a fire on a windy night and overflowing with passion. I jump into the flames and kiss him. His lips are swollen and plush. His slow, drugging kisses pull me deeper as my body roars with lust. The hand on my pelvis digs in as his free hand wraps around my face. Our kiss deepens, and I reach back and grab his ass. This is the first time I feel him shudder at my touch, and it instills a feeling of power within me.

"You are every fantasy that I have ever had," I say, my lips still touching his.

"Then let us put your fantasy to shame."

He spins me around so I am facing him. Both of his hands find my face as his fingers get lost in my hair. I close my eyes and just enjoy the feeling of him. He removes both hands and uses one finger to raise my chin. Instinctively, I open my eyes and watch as he looks over every inch of me.

"You are a goddess fallen from the skies above. I will feast on you until all the realms hear your cries of ecstasy." He kneels before me.

I slide my knees apart, giving him full access, and with a grin to rival Loki himself, he slides his tongue from clit to arse without losing eye contact. Everything below my belly button throbs with arousal. I lean back and grip the block as I press my dripping wet cunt into his face. He licks up every bit before sucking my clit into his mouth. The sensation wraps around my spine like a snake, making my toes curl.

"Your taste is as sweet as the first strawberries of the summer," he says, his lips glistening. He doesn't give me time to respond as he slides two fingers deep inside me and takes my clit back into his mouth.

"Fuuuuck."

"Mmmmm." His lips vibrate against my tender skin, causing my hips to buck. "I told you to hold on, sweetheart, and I wasn't lying. Hold still and let me give you your first orgasm of many."

I do my best to steady myself, but the tremble in my legs won't cease. He places a hand on my slick belly to aid me, but all it does is increase my arousal. His tongue swirls around my clit while his fingers unlock the code to my special spot. Every little movement raises me higher and higher. Tears burst from my eyes as my orgasm ripples through my body. I swear every cell in my body hums.

Before I can come down, his girth is inside of me. I arch my back, bringing him deep inside, and I press the top of my head into the block, getting as much leverage as I can. The sensation is almost unbearable, but I don't care. I want him. All of him.

"Fucking Hel, Princess, you feel even better than you taste," he says, his hands now on either side of mine and gripping just as tightly.

"I guess I'm not the only one who needs to hold on tight." I grin at him. He grins back before kissing me.

We stay frozen in this moment, kissing. Just the feel of him inside of me is enough, but the more we kiss the more, the moment shifts. Our hands move over each other's bodies in an attempt to memorize every inch. Each touch feels softer than the next, and while I thought we would be merely sharing a moment of physical desire, what was actually happening was much deeper.

He was tearing apart my broken soul and repairing it. I could feel something shifting in him, too.

Slowly he pumps in and out of me, letting me feel every inch. My pussy stretches and contracts to accommodate him, like it's welcoming him home. He stops kissing me and brushes a piece of hair off my forehead.

"I don't know what is happening, Brynja, but... this... you... are everything."

I can't think of anything appropriate to say, so I just press my forehead into his and recapture his lips.

He picks me up and I wrap my legs around his waist, his lips still fastened to mine. He sets me down in a soft pile of towels and continues to move in and out of me. I keep my legs wrapped around him, not wanting any space between us. Groans from deep within his chest finally fall from his lips and the sound alone threatens to push me over the edge again. There is something so sexy about a man letting himself go. Being primal.

"Mmmm. I love your moans," I whisper.

"Then you shall hear all of them."

REALM-SHATTERING MOANS. Countless orgasms. And one sunrise later—we finally part.

I thought I had known tiredness before, but I am not sure I can stand at this point. It doesn't help matters that

Booth is playing with my hair, making it exceedingly difficult to keep my eyes open.

"Why don't you stay here? With your family, with me…"

It is a sweet gesture and even though a large portion of me would wish for nothing more, I know I cannot.

"It is not safe for me to stay. The fact that I am still here now poses a threat to all of you."

"You know this city would fight for you, Princess."

"I do, but it is also something I do not wish to ask of them."

"Further proof you are an incredible woman," he says, tilting my chin up so that our eyes meet. "With a warrior's heart."

"Would a true warrior prolong danger merely to satisfy carnal urges?" I ask, smiling up at him.

"Abso-fucking-lutely."

I laugh. "You are just saying that to not taint last night."

"There is no way to taint last night, Princess." He peels himself away from me to grab our clothes. He pulls his trousers on before tossing me my own. I remain in place, just looking at the pile of clothes. They may as well be equivalent to a mountain at this moment.

"Can I at least escort you out of the city tonight? Be an extra set of eyes for a short while."

His comment about eyes reminds me of an important aspect of this journey I had forgotten. The seer! I immediately grab my clothes and put them on hastily.

"Why the sudden rush?" He smirks, still shirtless and looking far too appealing.

"I almost forgot, I must talk with the seer. Do you know her name, by chance?" I pull my tunic over my head.

"Apologies, Princess, but the seer has been dead for many years now."

A surprising amount of disappointment floods through me. I know even if I had talked to the seer there was no guarantee she could have told me anything, but at least it was an option. Now, I have nothing.

"Why do you seek a seer?"

Where to even begin with that question? There is so much in my life right now that is uncertain. One being where I will go. How will I live...

"I need answers. I honestly don't know where to begin, or end, for that matter."

"Would you like my thoughts?"

I nod. "I don't see how I could be any worse off..."

He sits beside me and twirls a ring on his pointer finger. His eyes focus on some point in the distance. "First, you must decide if you want to hide or fight." He turns his attention to me. "Once you have made that decision, the rest will fall into place."

Espen's voice plays in my head, telling me to fight. As much as I agree with him, how can I fight with merely Thyra and me? We are no match for the king. Even if I could sneak back into the castle and kill him where he slept, then what? There may be many who disagree with the king and his way of ruling, but there are plenty who do agree.

"That's it!" I say, realizing what I must do.

Booth smiles and leans back into the pile of towels. "Please tell me it involves you and me." He winks.

I smile and laugh, unable to ignore his charm. "No, you greedy man you. I know what I must do." I stand and pull on my trousers.

"And what, pray tell, is that?"

"I'm going to join the rebellion."

The expression on Booth's face completely changes as

panic sets in. "No, Princess, you can't do that. If they don't kill you themselves, they will turn you over to the king."

"Good thing I can be very persuasive," I say, putting all my gear back into place.

"You can't be serious."

"You told me I had to decide between hiding and fighting, and I choose to fight." I rest my beautiful new sword in my palm. "For my mother. For my brother and most importantly..." I pause, looking at my reflection in the steel. "For myself. He has taken everything from me. Now it is my turn to take *everything* from him!"

CHAPTER 10

Booth is still shouting at me as I return to Aunt Runy's. I must tell Thyra my decision and give her my thanks. As much comfort as her company has provided, I cannot, nor will I, ask her to come with me. I may have acted calm around Booth, but beneath the surface, I know his concerns are valid. The probability of them killing me on sight is high, but I cannot let that stop me. I have spent far too much of my life hiding and look what it brought me. I will not waste any more of it.

When I enter, Aunt Runy and Thyra are drinking coffee together at the table. They look like two old friends passing the time, which eases my thoughts of abandoning her. She has found a friend in Aunt Runy, and who could blame her? My aunt is wonderful. They both are.

"Where were you all night?" Thyra asks, side-eyeing me. She knows me far too well.

"I was patrolling."

"Then how come we have not seen you in hours? Your hair is awfully ruffled." Aunt Runy smiles, leaning back in her chair.

I skim my hand over my hair in hopes of smoothing it out. "Enough, you two. I have something important to say."

"Well, come sit and tell us what is so important that you didn't bother to wipe the sex off your face." Aunt Runy pats the chair beside her. It seems Thyra isn't the only one who can read me.

She leaves her chair to fetch me a cup. Once reseated, she fills the cup to the brim and I waste no time drinking half of it, not caring if I burn my tongue. The night of fun and no sleep is catching up with me. I also need a moment of calm before breaking the news. I know it will not be well received.

"Well?" Thyra asks, cup midway to her mouth.

"I'm... joining the rebellion," I say quickly, followed by a drink.

"When do we leave? I assume you will need some rest first. You look like you are about to collapse." Thyra doesn't miss a beat.

"You, my dear friend, will not be joining me."

"You have lost your mind if you think I would ever let you go alone. Absolutely not."

"And you have lost your mind if you think I would put you in danger."

"I don't nee—"

"Alright, that's enough." Aunt Runy says, slamming her hand on the table. "Correct me if I am wrong, but you are good friends, are you not?" We both nod. "And you are both grown women?" We nod again. "Then you can each make your own choice. Whether you agree or disagree is irrelevant."

"I wouldn't be able to bear it if something happened to you, Thyra." I turn my attention back to her. Aunt Runy is right, I just need her to understand my protest. "I have already lost my mother and my brother if I lost you... I... I don't know if I could handle it."

"And how do you think it would feel for me to lose you?" she asks, her eyes meeting mine. It pains me to even think it, but she is right. My feelings and desires are not the only thing at stake. "Would we not be better together?"

"I have no doubt you would be better together," Aunt Runy chimes in.

We look at Aunt Runy and then back at each other. No other words need to be spoken. It is understood. We will ride together. Now comes the hard part.

Finding the rebellion.

One main thing that has plagued the king in his battle against Sigvard and the rebellion is they never stay in one place. Attacking them is almost impossible. The king has far more resources than we do, but we have one thing he doesn't. Wit.

"Aunt Runy, where can I secure some maps?"

"Go to the square. There is a small blue shop on the north corner. A man named Telm owns it, and he sells everything from snakes to compasses. He will have what you need."

We exchange smiles before heading out the door.

The moment we are outside, Thyra questions me.

"Are you going to tell me what you were really up to last night, or are you going to leave me in suspense?"

My mind flashes back to last night. Goosebumps form all over my body, and I swear I can feel Booth's lips on mine again. I touch two fingers to my bottom lip just to be sure.

"Oh, please tell me!" Thyra darts in front of me, halting my forward momentum.

I smile and brush my hand over her long hair she has worn down since I made the comment.

"Some secrets are not meant to be shared," I tease her. I do want to tell her, but I also want to hold it close to my chest. Keep it just for me.

"Fine. I will just make up my own story then." She walks away, acting mad, but I know she is not. Just hungry for a little gossip.

The blue shop is exactly as Aunt Runy described. Small and somewhat hidden in the north corner of the square. If it was not blue, it would not be visible unless you knew what you were looking for. The door is slightly ajar and has a handwritten sign in the window that says open.

When we push open the door, the inside of the little shop is like a fantasy. There are shelves that rise from floor to ceiling and every one of them is filled. I walk to the closest shelf and let my eyes wander over each item. Some are familiar, like a horn hollowed out to enjoy a brew, but others are a mystery, including a weird-looking figurine. Moving closer, I squint my eyes to grasp what I am looking at, but it just looks like a many-armed woman dipped in tar. I reach out a finger to touch her when a voice stops me.

"I wouldn't touch her if I were you."

I turn to see a short, stout man in a green jumpsuit. His red hair and beard are immaculate and a sharp contrast against his light blue eyes. They are so light they almost look white. He is striking, to say the least.

"She has been known to throw around curses. I should really put her on a higher shelf."

"Oh!" I shriek while silently thanking the gods that I hadn't touched her. Thyra chuckles behind me.

"What can I help you find?"

I clear my throat and, hopefully, the embarrassment off my cheeks. "We require some maps."

"Ah! Wonderful! Lucky for you, I have plenty of those. Come. Follow me."

We follow him to the back of the store, where a giant table is covered with stuff. He snaps his fingers, and the table is completely clear.

"What in the world?!" Thyra's voice is shrill with confusion.

Telm must be an elf. I have heard of elves living among us, but they usually conceal their powers, just appearing as an average person. Telm seems to have no care for disguising who he truly is, but it makes me wonder why he would leave Alfheim, the realm of the elves, said to be more beautiful than the sun.

With a few waves of his hands, the table goes from empty to piled with stacks and stacks of what I assume are maps.

"What kind of map would you like?" He faces us.

I legitimately have no idea how to answer his question. A map is a... map.

"Well, a map of Midgard would be a good start."

"Midgard is much larger than you know, Princess. Why don't you tell me what you are looking for and I can help you narrow it down?"

I didn't realize Telm recognized me, and my cheeks flush all over again. "Please, call me Brynja, and I am looking for the impossible. Sigvard and his rebellion army."

"Then you need a very special kind of map. You came to the right person."

He shuffles through the piles until he pulls out a map

that is about the size of a handkerchief. He leans over so I can see but I see... nothing.

"Do you see anything?" I whisper to Thyra. She shakes her head no.

"Apologies, Telm, but I do not see a map."

"Good! Now hold it."

Confusion doesn't begin to describe my emotions, but I do as requested. The moment the map is in my hands, it comes to life. Mountains, lakes, and towns all start to appear one by one. There is even what appears to be a dragon in a cave! Mormor Thorsson always told me stories of a dragon in Fellheim, but I thought it was merely a tale.

"Wow! This is... incredible."

"What? What are you talking about? It's just an old piece of paper..." Thyra looks over my shoulder, eyebrows pulled together in confusion.

"You still can't see it?"

"No! See what?"

I hand her the map, and she turns it every which way, but the look of bewilderment on her face only deepens.

"Are you both jesting me?"

I take the map back and everything reappears.

"Only the owner of the map can see its details." Telm's eyes twinkle with mirth.

"But I am not the owner, you are."

"Not really. It never really liked me. Tolerated me at most. It clearly has been waiting for you."

I have no response but can't help the tickle of delight I feel in my belly. "Okay, so I have this... map. Now, how can I use it to find Sigvard?"

"Ask it!"

"He can't be serious," Thyra mumbles into my ear.

"I'm quite serious, but there is only one way to find out."

"What in Hel's name. Uhm... Map! Please show me the whereabouts of Sigvard and his army."

The images on the map begin to dance and swirl around like a tornado filled with glitter. Moments later, Fellheim becomes the focus of the map, its wide and various mountains covering almost the entire thing. To the north of the mountains, between their rocky edge and Lake Ravnvatn, is a large group of... dots?

I'm on the verge of confusion again when they start moving about and I see in the center of all the black dots there is one red one.

"Sigvard."

"Wait, you see him? This is not fair! Can I get my own magical map?" Thyra asks, her voice a mixture of annoyance and grouse. Telm merely chuckles at her.

"There are a few other things I would like to provide you with, if I may, Brynja."

I smile at him, feeling hopeful for the first time in a while. "That would be smashing."

When we leave Telm's lovely shop, we have everything we could need. He did give Thyra a map, just not a magical one. He also provided us with a compass, a few furs, and two cups. I tried to refuse the cups but he insisted.

Now we just have to wait for nightfall and our journey will begin. I can only hope it will not be our last. One thing I know for sure is that I need to sleep. I manage to make it to the bed Aunt Runy provided before my eyes fall closed.

What feels like moments later, I am being shaken awake. When my eyes open, the room is dark and I can only make out the shape of who has disturbed me.

"Come, Brynja. It's time."

I groan in displeasure but pull myself from the bed. Downstairs, Aunt Runy waits with a bowl of food and some water. I shake my head, but she presses the bowl into my hands.

"Please eat. You have a long journey and who knows when you shall eat again."

I do not want to eat but she is right. I need to start strong. The moment the food hits my lips, my body remembers it is hungry. I eat and drink every last bite before pulling Aunt Runy into a hug.

"Thank you for everything you have done for me."

"I would do it a thousand times over," she says, holding me tightly. She releases me and steps back, placing a hand on my shoulder. "Before you go, may I do one final act?"

I nod and she goes to the closet on the far side of the room. When she returns, she has what looks like a paintbrush and a jar of ink. She signals for me to sit, and I do.

"This ink isn't permanent, but your Mormor would disagree. I painted something on her cheek while she slept, and it remained there for well over a year."

I laugh. "What did you paint on her?" The cool brush moves across my cheekbone just below my left eye.

"Let's leave that in the past," she chuckles.

"Then how can I trust you will not do the same to me?"

"You would agree it's too late, would you not?" She sets the brush down. "All done. Now you will have protection wherever your journey takes you."

I pick up a plate from the table and look at my reflection. The Viking rune for protection is now perfectly marked on my skin.

I hug her one more time, and while still embraced, she whispers into my ear. "Mormor would have been so proud of you."

I leave before the tears fall. I have cried enough. From now on, only blood will flow.

I join Thyra outside. She is already seated on her horse. I'm about to mount up when I hear a voice shouting my name. When I turn, I see Booth walking toward us.

I did not think this man could get any more tantalizing, but phew!

He is wearing a tight, long-sleeved pale blue tunic with a metal vest over the top. Leather bracers are wrapped around his wrist almost up to his elbows, and he has matching leather leg guards. Every hard line of him is clearly visible yet covered at the same time. Two swords are jutting up from his back and he has a fur tied around his waist. It matches the flaming color of his eyes.

"And what do you think you are doing?" Thyra asks since I am unable to form words at the moment.

"What kind of gentlemen would I be if I didn't escort two ladies out of town in the dead of night?" He places his hand behind his head and purposely flexing.

"So, you are merely escorting us? Not tagging along?" Thyra remains unpleased by his presence.

"I know where I belong, and as much as I don't like you two going alone, it is not my place." He smiles and I watch as his eyes dance with enjoyment. "It seems the princess has lost her ability to speak."

I clear my throat and do my best to look at him without drooling. "I was merely letting you two hash it out. Are we ready to proceed now?"

He snickers but does not say another word, so we ride.

It doesn't take long for us to reach the edge of Thora. It is one of the many reasons I love it here. A smaller town, with a slow aura but deep passions. The complete opposite of the palace and the surrounding area. Everything there felt so… forced. Fake. Except for Vildmark, which will never be the same now without Espen or Agnarr. I wonder if I will ever see him again.

"Brynja, are you going to get your head out of the clouds so you can say goodbye to your lovah?" Thyra asks, emphasizing the "ah" to make it sound extra sultry.

"Yes, why don't you ride a bit farther and give us some privacy," Booth says to Thyra but winks at me.

She sighs and rolls her eyes. "Just don't take long. We don't have all night." She rides off far enough that I can no longer hear her horse's hooves.

"I am truly going to miss you, Princess." He looks off into the distance while petting his horse's neck. I jump down and walk over to him. I wrap my hand around his cheek and he presses it into my palm.

"I will miss you as well." I plunge my hand into his hair. His free hand wraps around my wrist before planting a kiss on it.

"You are exceptional. Never doubt that."

"I will do my best."

He pulls me into his body and kisses me. It's a kiss so sensual and consuming that I fear it may be my last. If it is, my only regret is that I didn't get to see what more it could be.

CHAPTER 11

"I knew it!" Thyra giggles.

My horse strides up beside hers and they fall in sync, walking slowly down the long path in front of us. The journey already felt overbearing, but leaving Thora and Booth behind feels even heavier. There is no longer anything between us and Sigvard.

"You truly aren't going to say anything?" Thyra's words bring me out of my somber mood and back into my night with Booth. The mere thought of his hands on my skin causes goosebumps to cover my entire body.

"It was... phenomenal."

"Better than Agnarr?"

No immediately comes to my mind, but I pause and pretend to think, not wanting to insult my relationship with Agnarr any further than I already have. It also isn't fair to compare them. I have known Agnarr all my life, I don't even know Booth's last name. *Real princess-like, Brynja...*

"Well?" Thyra asks impatiently.

"They were very different experiences, Thyra, and I'd prefer not to think about Agnarr at this moment."

"Of course..." By the way she trails off, she isn't done probing me. Instead of humoring her, I decide to wait it out. I wonder, is Espen the only man she has ever been with? "Are you going to make me beg for details?"

I smile. "I will not if you answer a question for me first."

"What is it?"

"Is Espen the only man you have been with?"

A beautiful, tender smile shimmers on her lips. "Yes. He was."

Her words jab the knife already in my heart a touch deeper. I trace my fingers down my horse's muscular yet soft neck in an attempt to find any sort of relief.

"But I would have been doing Agnarr, Booth, Arik, and Aksel if I had the chance. You have to remember I lived a life without any say. Espen was my only flicker of freedom."

Aksel and Astrid! How could I have forgotten to say goodbye to the twins? I will have to find a way to send word to them. Wait...

"You think Aksel is attractive? And Arik? The man I am supposed to marry?" I can't even begin to hide the shocked expression on my face. Thyra and I spoke freely about many things, but clearly, she kept some to herself as well.

"Aksel is okay, just one of the first names I could think of, but Arik, he was good-looking. Do you not agree?"

"I think my mind was more focused on the fact that I was being forced to marry, but I do remember his eyes. They were beautiful."

She laughs lightly.

"Now if you would be so kind. Tell me what happened with Booth and spare no detail."

It takes us until morning to reach the base of Fellheim. The mountain and what awaits on the other side hang heavy and ominous in the air. I can even feel it on my skin. There is a path to follow up the mountainside, but only Odin knows how far it will truly take us. We say a prayer to the gods and begin our ascent.

By midafternoon, we have dismounted the horses and are walking. The temperature isn't overly hot, but the sun is blazing down on us and there is no shade except for an occasional tree.

"What have we gotten ourselves into?" Thyra asks, wiping sweat off her forehead.

"The only way over a mountain is to climb it." I pass her the water.

"Why couldn't we wait until they moved to someplace more accessible?"

"I doubt they will be moving from their location anytime soon. They have the perfect setup. Mountains blocking one side and a lake at their back."

"Well, this mountain is kicking my arse. Around the next turn, I am taking a rest."

I nod in agreement as my calves have been screaming for the last half mile.

When we make it around the next turn, there is a poor excuse for a tree providing the smallest bit of reprieve from the sun. The problem is, it is already occupied.

"What is that?" Thyra squints, trying to make sense of the blue blob.

"Perhaps it's just a colorful rock?" I move closer, not even believing myself.

I have only made it a few steps closer when the blob

uncurls and stretches. It has many features of a cat, the first being its large ears like the hairless cats from the deserts far to the south, but it is not hairless. Quite the opposite. It has long silky hair that flows down its body like a waterfall and changes from blue to green at the base of its tail. The green tail is double the length of its body and three times as fluffy. Just when I was beginning to think it was cute, I notice its paws. Both front paws have white and green claws that look like they could rip open a chest in one strike. On top of its head is a crown of feathers that are vibrant blue. Whatever it is... it's eerily beautiful.

Thyra, seeming not to care about its beauty or potential danger, moves under the small slice of shade directly beside it. It sits unblinking, looking at her as she rummages around in her sack before pulling out an orange. She begins peeling and eating slices completely unfazed by the blue cat monster.

The cat...thing tilts its head sideways, and before I can suggest she rethink her location, it swiftly opens its tail. A gorgeous display of green and blue feathers surrounds it and knocks Thyra on her backside. At that moment, I realize its tail looks exactly like a peacock. The creature is a catcock. I snicker and it glares at me.

"Not only do you disturb my slumber, but you laugh at me. You must have a death wish. Now, who are you?"

"Apologies, ummm, catco..." I pause, knowing the moment I say catcock out loud, I will not be able to keep a straight face. I take a breath and start again. "I mean no disrespect. What is your name?"

"I will tell you once you explain to me who you are and why you are here."

"I am Brynja and this is my dear friend Thyra. We are on our way—"

"To join Sigvard. Of course. My apologies, Princess, I should have recognized you."

I am at a loss for words. The catcock not only knows me but knows my plans? How?

"How did you know of our plans? We have not spoken a word to anyone outside of Thora!"

"It is my job to know everything, and we have been waiting for you. Come."

We?

I glance over at Thyra. She is still happily eating her orange as if this is completely normal.

"Thyra..."

"I'm choosing to live in momentary bliss before the cat feather duster and his friend kill us."

"We would never harm Princess Brynja or anyone she deems worthy of her company. Perhaps I should introduce myself and it will make you feel more at ease. My name is Alfvin and I live in these mountains, providing protection to those who dwell below. It is a long journey over the mountains, and we would like to offer you a... quicker solution."

"And who is the other half of this we?" Thyra asked, eyebrow raised as she chewed on the last bit of orange.

"If you come with me, you can meet her for yourself."

Sweat rolls down my back. Sol, the sun goddess, is showing off today. My calves have stopped screaming but they have not forgotten. At this moment, the risk is worth the reward. We don't have much water left so I do what any sane thirsty person would do. Follow the catcock.

Just when I'm starting to believe this whole thing is a mirage and I may keel over from heat exhaustion, Alfvin stops in front of a giant bolder. I would cry but I am pretty sure there is no fluid left in my body.

"Now what?" Thyra asks, her voice barely audible over her heavy breathing.

Before I can formulate an answer, Alfvin knocks on the bolder and it slides open just wide enough for us to fit through. Alfvin dashes inside, but Thyra and I remain standing in place, mesmerized.

His fluffy head reappears and he uses his tail to wave us over. "Come. Get inside and out of the heat."

Thyra and I clasp hands and walk into the dark entrance.

The cool air from the cave swirls around me, providing instant relief after hours in the sun. I don't even care that I can't see anything around me.

Alfvin circles my ankles before saying, "This way."

I have no idea how he expects me to follow him in utter darkness, but then a small light appears. It is dancing side to side just like a lightning bug flying around in a field of tall grass. Alfvin must have a light on the tip of his tail. Thyra and I do our best to keep up without falling, following the tiny dot of light.

In an instant, the darkness completely fades, and we are in a beautiful room. A chandelier hangs in the center that is covered with ocean-colored gemstones. The light reflecting off the gems gives the illusion of the room being underwater. Below the chandelier is what appears to be a bed comprised of hay and Alfvin's feathers. The bed is huge.

"Magnus, our guests have arrived," Alfvin bellows.

I'm not prepared for what comes around the corner.

Magnus matches the colors of the stones in the chandelier with touches of alternating shades of purple throughout her body. Her nails appear to be black but when the light hits them just right, they shimmer with purples and teals. She bends her head down so we are at eye level. I can see my entire form in the depths of her pupil. Under other circumstances, I would be terrified but there is something tender in her eyes. That and her iris color is breathtaking. It is the most stunning shade of violet.

"Princess Brynja, it is my pleasure to finally meet you."

"You are real. I thought Mormor was just telling me bedtime stories."

"Alva was an amazing woman."

I have only heard Mormor's first name used one other time, when Morfar was pissed at her. I already knew she was the most fascinating person I had ever met, and her being friends with a dragon just solidified that.

"How did you meet?"

Magnus laughs, causing the entire room to shake. "Out of all the questions you could ask, that is the one you chose?"

"Wouldn't you want to know if our roles were reversed?"

A smirk pulls at both sides of her mouth. "Alva would be proud."

A wave of grief crashes over me, filled with all the memories of Mormor, but not just her. Espen and my mother. I do my best to smile back at Magnus while pushing down the heartache.

Magnus's chest glows bright fuchsia, giving the entire cave a pinkish hue before picking me up into her arms and smashing me against her chest.

"I am so sorry for your loss, Princess. I can't imagine the grief you are feeling, but know Alva, Espen, and Anitra would be proud of you."

I am not sure if I should laugh or cry. Magnus's chest is so warm a sheen of sweat has formed instantly on my skin.

Her claw is also completely wrapped around my body and all it would take is one squeeze to turn me into bone dust.

"Thank you, Magnus, but would you mind putting me down?"

She chuckles and Thyra vibrates across the floor like a bean inside of a lyre. She does, however, set me gently back on the ground.

"Come! Let's eat!"

We follow Magnus through another dark hallway when we come to a beautiful dining room. I truly should not be surprised any longer. I have met a catcock and a dragon and found a secret mountain bedroom. Why wouldn't there be a secret dining area as well?

A similar chandelier hangs in the center of the room ,but instead of gems the color of the ocean, they are an array of purples. The giant wood table below it has enough food to feed an entire army, and I can't decide where to begin.

"We were unsure what kind of food you would prefer, so we made everything!" Alfvin says with a big grin on his face.

"You did not need to go through all this trouble. I have not encountered a food I do not enjoy." I walk around the table, eyeballing every delicious morsel available.

Thyra is already seated, adding an assortment of delectable goodies to her plate. She has only ever seen offerings this grand but has never been allowed to partake. The servants were lucky if they got fruit. Their meals were consistently stew and bread due to the ability to make them in mass quantities with ease.

I watch as Thyra takes a big bite of what appears to be roasted duck. She chews it slowly with her eyes closed, savoring every second before swallowing it down with a sip of red wine.

"You should eat too, Princess. You will need your strength for all that is to come," Magnus whispers over my shoulder.

I take a few more moments living in Thyra's joy before sitting beside her.

"You have to try this duck, it is succulent." She smiles, her lips shiny with grease.

"Yes, please."

Thyra adds some to my plate. Magnus sits at the head of the table with Alfvin to her right. He makes a plate for her before taking care of himself. I expect Magnus to devour it all in one bite, but she picks up a fork and knife and cuts herself small bites. My mother would be absolutely delighted. Pain wrings my heart, but I am also curious. Did she know Magnus or was Mormor the only one?

"Did you know my mother?" I fight back the urge to cry and force myself to focus on the fact that I am having dinner with a dragon and a catcock.

"I did not. Alva was the only one we trusted." My face must show my sorrow as Magnus's expression shifts and her chest glows pink again. "I have many sublime tales about Alva, if you would like to hear them."

"I would love that," I say, taking a bite of the duck. The meat melts in my mouth and I manage to contain the moan of satisfaction from escaping, but my stomach growls for more. Not eating and climbing a mountain has me famished.

"She saved me," Magnus starts abruptly, piquing my attention. "My mother was killed too, but when I was a baby. I was left alone in a harsh world. One where people only wanted to keep me imprisoned and to use me as a weapon."

Her words are all too familiar. Visions of my father flash through my mind and all the times he imprisoned me.

"I thought I would never escape, and I prayed for a battle where I could die with some sort of dignity. And then Alva found me. Not only did she find me, she used her magic to make my captors forget I even existed."

Magic? As a lach, she had gifted healing powers, but that doesn't sound at all like what Magnus is referring to.

"What do you mean, she used her magic? Did she have more than just healing powers?"

"Much more. Alva was very powerful. She saved all of Thora from the great flood without giving any inkling of her true identity."

"Are you saying Mormor was a seer?"

Magnus merely nods as if she didn't just drop a giant secret into my unsuspecting lap.

"Why would she hide that?" I feel like I didn't truly know her.

"She loved being a lach. Healing people brought her such... fulfillment. There are also those who do not value seers. Her reputation was more important to her than her abilities."

"I just wish she had told me. I would have kept her secret."

"She wanted to. Many times. Yet she feared it would put you in more danger."

I'm overwhelmed with emotions. The biggest was the feeling of not truly knowing Mormor. That even around me, she didn't feel comfortable enough to be completely exposed. Magnus's chest glows a deep gray as pain pulls at the corner of her eyes.

"No one knew Alva better than you, Princess. I may have known her secret, but it was because she risked everything to save me and she only asked me for one thing in return."

"What was it?" Thyra asks, refilling her wine.

"That I protect Brynja when the time comes."

"Has the time come?" I ask as my heart skips a beat.

"It is on the horizon."

I knew the risks when I left the palace. What I didn't expect was it getting so grim I would require a dragon's assistance to keep me from the afterlife. I grab the bottle of wine Thyra has been hoarding and fill my glass to the brim. With death breathing down my neck, I will enjoy every moment I have left.

THE NEXT TIME I open my eyes, I am wedged between Magnus and Thyra. I am so sweaty from the heat radiating off of Magnus that I have to use great effort to remove myself from her side. When I free myself, the momentum required sends me rolling down the bed and onto the floor. Thankfully, the floor offers a refreshing reprieve from the gates of Niflheim I just managed to escape, so I don't bother to get up.

"Her heat is overwhelming in the summer, but come winter it's a blessing," a voice says from overhead. I open one eye and see Alfvin standing over me. "Come. I have something to show you."

Regrettably, I pull myself up from the floor and follow Alfvin.

He leads me down another long dark pathway, and if I hadn't already survived the night, I would fear death was upon me. We reach a small room that is almost empty aside from some large boxes stacked in the corner. Alfvin walks over to the boulder on the far side of the room and, just as before, he slides it out of the way. I step into the light, and as the wind swirls around me, I see the world below.

We are now on the back side of the mountain, and the sun glistens off Lake Ravnvatn. Between us and the lake are thousands of tents. I can't make out any details from this distance, but based on the map from Telm, this is Sigvard and the resistance.

"Here," Alfvin says, handing me a pair of binoculars.

The binoculars give me a closer glimpse of the camp. It appears to be mostly men with a few women sprinkled in. I wish I could get closer, and just as I finish my thought, the binoculars zoom in closer.

I lower the binoculars to inspect them but do not see anything unusual. I turn and look at Alfvin. "Is anything around here not magical?"

"The bed?"

I laugh and bring the binoculars back to my eyes. I move around the area until I stop on three men walking the camp together. Two of them appear to be flanking the man in the center.

The sides of his head are shaved, but the middle section of his dark brown hair is about finger length and messy. He has a full beard climbing up the sides of his cheeks and a tattoo wrapped around his neck. He has on a long sleeve tunic but one sleeve has been removed. The arm that is exposed is completely covered in tattoos.

"Sigvard?" I ask, turning back to Alfvin. He nods.

I watch him move about the camp. He is clearly respected and cares about his men. He would not walk around camp and tend to them all if he didn't. The king would never walk among his men. If they wished to speak with him, they had to come to his tent on their knees. Sigvard is engaging. Strong. What is he hiding?

I hand the binoculars back to Alfvin, and we return to the main room of the cave. Magnus and Thyra are awake. Thyra's hair stands straight up like she was struck by a thunderbolt.

"Thyra, are you attempting a new hairstyle? I am not sure I am partial to it."

She reaches up and feels her hair is sticking straight up. She rolls her eyes and slams her bowl to the ground.

"You told me it looked fine!" she yells at Magnus.

"It does look fine."

"This is not fine, Magnus. I look like Thor attempted to kill me with one of his thunderbolts."

She pulls a brush out of her bag and attempts to return her hair to its normal state.

"Should I even ask how?" I cover my mouth to hide my smile.

"I woke up all sweaty and my hair was soaked. Magnus offered to dry it and she blasted me with her hot dragon breath. I was worried it looked like a mess, but she assured me it looked fine." We all laugh except for Thyra. "It's not funny. Imagine if I walked into the rebel camp looking like that."

"I would have never allowed that to happen, but how did you not feel it?"

"I don't know! I just thought it was all on the top of my head." She throws the brush back in her bag. She now has her hair perfectly braided. "Can we go? I'm ready to get off this fucking mountain."

Thyra doesn't curse often, only when she is pissed, which is rare. She has such a sweet soul, so now I feel partially bad for laughing at her, but that memory will live with me forever. Equally, I needed it. Without some sort of joy, I would be drowning in sorrow. The one other thing keeping me going is the rebellion. The king will pay for what he did.

"It would be my pleasure to give you a ride down to the camp," Magnus says.

"Your offer is appreciated, but my arrival will already be unfavorable. Adding you to the mix could result in bloodshed."

"Understood, Princess. At least let me take you down to the base of Fellheim, out of sight. You will need all your strength for battle."

I nod. "It is time."

The flight down is quick, and I find myself missing the sky the moment my feet touch the ground. It is so freeing being one with the wind. Magnus and Alfvin bid us farewell, and we start the short trek to the camp. The smell of blood and salt thickens in the air with each step we take. The moment we break from the trees, I feel all the eyes on us. My heart thrums in my chest as I take deep breaths to steady myself. We have made it this far, but that doesn't mean an arrow isn't aimed for my chest somewhere in the distance.

Just as we reach the edge of the camp, Sigvard and the two men I saw march toward us. I attempt to find any other emotion on his face, but all I can see is rage. My palm twitches to reach for my sword, but if I do that, a war will break out. My war is not with Sigvard. It is with the king.

I expect him to stop several feet from me, to keep a safe distance, but he does not. He walks right up to me so we are face to face. He has not spoken yet, but I can feel his breath on my neck. In my core, I am scared. This is not a man to mess with, but in my heart, where Espen and my mother still live, there is an unwavering strength.

"State your name before I kill you." Sigvard's voice is deep and menacing.

"Brynja. Hallstrom," I say, my voice steady and strong.

Gasps arise from the crowd gathering behind us, and swords are pulled from their scabbards.

Chapter 12

He backs up slightly and looks me up and down before laughing. "Oh Princess, you are in the wrong place. Go before I send your head back to your father," he says, turning on his heels.

"I didn't know you did his bidding. He would be happy to receive my head. One less burden." I grind my teeth together in anger. I feel Thyra's hand on my shoulder, but I will not let this man treat me as if I am nothing.

Sigvard turns back around. "You truly have a death wish, aye, Princess. I didn't become the leader of this rebellion by being foolish. There is word everywhere of him requesting your whereabouts. So, I can either send you back to him in pieces or you can walk out of here. Your choice."

I stride up to him and place my hand in the center of his chest. A vision ripples through me of Sigvard covered in blood with a head in either hand. I blink my eyes firmly to clear the vision, not wanting it to take hold.

The two men on either side of him reach for their swords, but he holds out a hand. I trail my hand up his chest and wrap it around his neck, pulling him as close to me as possible. Countless images of Sigvard flicker through my mind, causing me to have to speak through gritted teeth.

"Go ahead and kill me, then, because there is no way I am going back willingly." I release his neck and step back before dropping to my knees in front of him.

The man to his right pulls out his sword and steps forward. "Let me kill her, Sigvard. It would bring me great pleasure."

I raise my chin and tilt my head to expose my neck.

"Brynja, please," Thyra whimpers behind me. I had briefly forgotten about her presence, but I did not come all this way, finally escaping my own prison, to be turned away.

"Turn away, Thyra. You do not need to see this."

"Sparing your servant, how kind of you," the man with the sword says while sticking the blade into the recess of my neck.

Thyra drops to her knees beside me and grabs my hand. "I am not her servant. I am her friend and as her friend, I will not let her die alone."

I bite my tongue to halt the shift in my emotions. I will not show weakness in front of Sigvard, no matter how sweet the gesture. I will also not allow this. Thyra is finally free. She will not die by my side for no true cause. I turn my gaze so our eyes meet.

"It is not your time, my friend. You have sacrificed enough for me."

"Brynja, get off your knees and fight this asshole."

Thrya's mouth is moving, but the words are not hers. It

is a male voice. A very familiar male voice. Espen. I go to speak his name when I hear his voice again.

"Do not speak to me out loud, they will deem you insane. Use your mind. What are you doing sacrificing yourself to this asshole?"

"He won't kill me."

"How do you know that?"

"My brother taught me."

"Good. Now get off your knees and show him who you truly are."

"I miss you so much it hurts."

I WAIT for a reply but there is nothing. Just as quickly as he came, he is gone. If he was even really here. I have no notion of what is true anymore. Between the visions, meeting a dragon, and now hearing Espen, I may truly be losing my grip. I am also kneeling in front of a known killer, challenging him not to kill me.

I turn my attention back to Sigvard. He still stands in front of me. His counterpart slowly drives the tip of his blade deeper into my neck, and Thyra grips my hand so tightly I have lost feeling.

"Thyra, loosen your hold on me. It will not alter our fate."

Sigvard's eyes meet mine for the first time. They are a deep shade of green so dark they almost look black. It seems he expected me to flinch, to recoil in fear, but I never did that with the king. I will not give him the satisfaction either.

"Henrik, remove your blade from her throat."

"Sigvard, you ca—"

"Do not quarrel with me, or you will be the one to go to Valhalla."

Henrik reluctantly removes his blade and storms off. Sigvard holds out his hand to me and helps me to my feet.

"Do not take this as an invitation, I just need to know how you found me."

I can't help that smile that comes to my face. "It wasn't difficult."

"Keep pushing, Princess, and your head will be on a silver platter. Come this way, before the entire camp sees you."

Sigvard walks a short distance across the camp to a large tent in the far corner. I would have expected him to be in the center but so would any commander. Smart. Inside, the tent is riddled with maps and supplies, everything from swords to bread. I can't imagine food is easy to come by unless they hunt or raid.

He takes a seat behind the table and tosses back whatever liquid is left in the bloody wooden goblet. "Now, tell me how you were able to find my camp but the great king was not."

"He is not as cunning as I, nor can he see beyond his own nose," I say, resisting the urge to cross my arms with frustration.

He laughs and pulls an apple out from somewhere and tosses it into the air. "I have to admit, not the response I was expecting. Are you and Daddy in a big fight or what?" He jabs the apple with his knife in midair.

There is a part of me that wants to tell him everything to prove his ignorant arse wrong, but my personal affairs are none of his fucking business.

"All you need to know is I do not consider him my father. Here is merely the king and not a very good one."

"And you just expect me to take you at your word?" He bites into the apple, the juice dripping down his lip.

I understand his hesitation, but I'm over this intimidation game.

"Yes, I do. Why would I risk walking in here?"

"To do exactly this. Earn my trust, lull me into lowering my guard... and then slit my throat in my sleep."

He leans back, the apple forgotten, eyes narrowing as if he's already weighed every version of this moment.

"I'm sorry, Princess. But you're going in the cage."

The words land like a slap.

"What—"

I don't get the rest out.

Three men step into the tent like shadows called by command. I want to fight, but I don't. What's the point? Even if I broke free, there's an entire camp out there—and not one of them will let me walk.

So I don't scream. I don't swing.

I let them drag me to the cage like I belong there.

Thyra is imprisoned as well but in a different cage out of shouting range. I wonder if she regrets her choice to be by my side. We have merely gone from one prison to the next.

There is nothing in the cage but dirt and, based on the blood, I am far from the first person to be thrown in here. I attempt to find a way to lean against the cage comfortably but nothing I do works. I opt to lie flat on my back with my hands cupped behind my head. The sky is clear with a cool breeze blowing off the lake, so I close my eyes and imagine I am back in Thora.

I can hear Mormor's voice calling me home for supper. I would spend all day splashing around in the water and looking for frogs. Mormor told me if I ever found a frog with purple legs to capture it for her. She said he had special healing properties that she could use to save people. I was determined to find it for her but never did. I even tried to trick her by painting one purple, but paint does not stick to frogs. I wonder now if that story was true. Just like Magnus. I, of course, believed it when I was a child, but as an adult, I grew to just think of it as a fond memory. It didn't matter if it was true or not.

Gods, I miss her. Why do all the pieces of my heart have to be shattered?

"I thought Sigvard was spewing dung, but here you are. In the flesh."

Great. Someone else to taunt me. I remain still, willing myself back to my memories.

He chuckles. "I wouldn't talk to me either, just know we don't all agree with you being caged like an animal."

This makes me laugh. All I've heard throughout my life are reasons why I should be caged. The notion that anyone would think otherwise is laughable.

"Will you at least tell me what is so amusing?"

I curse under my breath and force myself into a seated position, leaning against the cage. Outside, leaning against the bars stands a tall man with long dark blonde hair with strong ash tones and honey-freckled eyes. Half of his hair is pulled back so it is out of his vision and the rest falls past his collarbone. He has scruff on his face, leaving me to wonder how he manages a shave out here, and a devilishly handsome smile. He is shirtless, with only a full arm guard on his right arm and a piece of leather crossing his chest to hold the sword at his back. A tattoo scales over his shoulder and expands over his strongly defined chest muscle. Sweat is dripping down the center of his abs. Sigvard must have sent him here as a test.

I laugh again and look away. I can't deny his appearance is alluring, but I am not here to tame heathens. I am here to fight. He walks closer, wraps his hands around the bars, and appears to look me up and down, but it's hard to tell without looking at him directly.

"Pleased to see your spirits aren't broken."

"As if you truly care about my spirits. Be gone. You have seen the freak show, now go about your business."

"How about I stay and you tell me why you are truly here?"

I stand up and walk over to him, wrapping my hands around his. "I'd rather die."

His eyes shift back and forth over my facial features, "Spoken like a true warrior." He removes his hands from under mine and begins to walk away before pausing. "I would consider at least telling Sigvard something because if you don't, you will get your wish."

"May I ask you something?"

He turns back and nods.

"Did anyone else have to sing for their supper?"

He shakes his head.

"Then why should I?"

A small smirk forms at the corner of his mouth before he departs.

I spend the remainder of the day listening to the sounds of metal clashing and grunts of victory from some of Midgard's most dangerous warriors. I had questioned coming here and even though I am currently locked up with the key thrown away, I know I am where I was destined. My purpose is to fight alongside the people of the rebellion.

By nightfall, the air has cooled significantly, and the camp has fallen silent. I expected fighting by day and celebration by night, but the only sound is the wind. I lie on my back counting the stars, hoping to find Espen and my mother among them.

"Missing the comforts of the palace yet, Princess?"

I can already recognize Sigvard's voice, and I have no desire to see him, let alone speak to him. For someone who was imprisoned, you would think it would be the last thing he would want to do to others, but it appears he views it as the ultimate revenge. I close my eyes and wish for Thor to strike him dead. Instead, I hear him urinating. The smell is strong against the dry dirt and the sound has brought the reminder of how thirsty I am.

"Sleep well, Princess," he guffaws.

Once he is out of sight, I use my boot to kick some dirt over his foul-smelling urine before closing my eyes and escaping into the dreamworld.

Sleep doesn't last long. Between the brisk air and lying on the hard ground, my back is screaming. Instead, I pace the length of the cage, hoping to calm my back and warm my body. The full moon reflects off the lake as the sound of tree frogs echoes across the camp.

I halt my movements when I hear banging noises, but the camp remains still. I take a few steps when it happens again, but this time I know exactly where it is coming from—Thyra's cell. I can see her but can't determine what she is using to alert me or where she acquired it. She is, however, doing something with her hands. I don't have the slightest idea what.

I shake my head, but she continues to sign with her hands frantically. Even if I knew sign language, the moon is providing only enough light to make out basic forms. It's impossible to figure out what she is attempting to tell me. I make an exaggerated shrug, and she throws whatever it was that she used to alert me. Clearly, she is disheartened.

"What are you two fighting about?"

I turn around, surprised, and my eyes land on the long-haired man from before. He is donning the same clothing, if you can call what he has on clothing, and holding an apple in each hand. He tosses one to me before taking the second one over to Thyra. I am still looking at the apple in disbelief when he returns. Orn brought me an apple the last time I was imprisoned.

"I know it's not much, but I would still suggest eating it. Looking at it will provide you nothing."

"Orn used to bring me apples." The words fall out of my mouth before I can stop them.

"Who is Orn?"

I shake my head, hoping to clear away my vulnerability, and bite into the apple.

"If you aren't going to speak to me, I am just going to make up my own stories."

"Have you considered introducing yourself? Why would I share any sort of information with a stranger when I do not even know their name?"

He smiles that devilishly handsome smile again before pulling his sword from his scabbard. My breath catches momentarily until he places it down on the ground. He walks away from the sword, sits against the cage, and pats the dirt. My eyes remain locked on him, uncertain if I truly want to sit that close to him.

"Come, Brynja. Sit. I will not harm you."

The use of my name and the kindness in his voice sway me. I sit against the cage with my back in line with his. We sit silently. The warmth of his presence pulls the chills from my bones, swallows some of my loneliness. It seems no matter where I find myself, I'm always on the outside looking in.

"Name's Sten." He leans his head back and his hair sways across my neck. "Sigvard and I came from the same slave house. I took the fall for my family after raiding a farmer's field. I couldn't stand to see my sister so frail..."

"How long has it been since you have seen your family?"

"Three years."

It has only been a week since I lost Mother and Espen, but it feels like two lifetimes. I can't imagine what three years apart feels like.

"Do you regret it?"

"Never," he says, running his hands through the dry dirt. "I knew the risks, and it was either all of us die of starvation or I become a slave."

"Do you know if they are still alive?" I create a mountain of dirt between my thighs.

"No." He lapses into silence, his hands becoming still. I can only hope the king didn't kill them, but I don't have high hopes. I will not voice this to Sten, however. "I have never lost hope of seeing them again and when Sigvard joined the house, I knew change was coming."

I'm intrigued by Sten. How he has managed not to lose himself in such harsh circumstances. How he still has such a kind heart. I am still not convinced he is not here at Sigvard's request, but his kindness cannot be ignored.

"I'm sorry for what the king did to you."

"Do not be sorry. I was destined to be here. The journey may have been disagreeable, but I would not change it. The gods have blessed me." I nod even though Sten cannot see me. "Princess Brynja, are you going to finally tell me why you are here?"

My breath hitches in my chest. I wrap my hand tightly

around Espen's necklace and pray to hear his voice again, but nothing.

"You have no reason to trust me, just as I have no reason to trust you, but we can't begin to build trust unless you speak," Sten says.

"You truly want to know?"

I feel him nod. I face him. If he wants the truth, I want him to look me in my eyes and see my pain and still try to call me a liar, because I know he will.

"Look at me first."

He turns and our eyes meet. I wrap my hands around the bars and press my face as close to him as my confinement will allow.

"The king killed my mother and my brother. I... am here for revenge."

A single tear rolls down my cheek as I wait for him to tell me lies will get me nowhere.

"I will make sure you are released as soon as the sun rises," he says, wrapping both hands tightly around mine.

I would cry but I am too relieved to shed any more tears. I may not be able to convince Sigvard that my presence here is favorable, but Sten can.

CHAPTER 13

- Sigvard

The sun rose many hours ago, but I remain in bed. Henrik has been chomping at the bit to kill the princess, but I'm certain she has valuable information we must obtain first. Torturing her would most certainly loosen her tongue, but the consequences could be dire. I also take no pleasure in torturing a woman, regardless of who she is.

"Sigvard, would you put your dick away already? Half the day has been wasted."

Some days, I question why I've kept Henrik by my side. He's as dense as a stump and smells like week-old rot—but he'd gut anyone who so much as looked at me wrong. Finn at least has half a brain, not that it's his fault. His mother abandoned him when he was just days old. He has been passed around from house to house since then.

"Sigvard!"

"Shut your fucking mouth, you impatient arse."

"Sten has been waiting to have words with you since sunrise."

Why the fuck didn't he just say that? I run a hand over my face and find my feet. The chill from the night has worn off. Sol has been performing her job too well as of late, but the lake at our backs has proven beneficial in numerous ways, including as a reprieve from the heat. I don't bother with a tunic and just don trousers. My trusty blades hang off either hip.

When I emerge, Sten is standing near the tent opening, looking out. He appears tormented. He was on guard last night, which immediately catches my attention.

"Sten," I say, approaching arm out. He claps my forearm tightly and provides a weak smile. "What is it, brother?"

"I fear you will not like what I have to say."

"Only one way to know. Out with it."

He releases my forearm and sits on the stool in the corner of the room. "You should release the princess."

A roar of laughter flies from my chest. "You must be sleep-deprived, the princess is not going anywhere but Niflheim."

"And I'm going to do it," Henrik chimes in.

"You wouldn't even give her the dignity of Valhalla?"

Another bout of laughter trembles through my body. "Only warriors go to Valhalla. Go. Sleep. Before you make any more ridiculous claims."

He gets up and closes the distance between us. "You might want to actually speak with her before making such decisions."

He walks out of the tent before I can speak.

"Sten has a weak heart. Do not listen to him, Sigvard,"

Finn says from behind me. The man has the unsettling habit of sneaking up on people.

"All men have a weakness, whether they are aware of it or not." My eyes are still locked on where Sten once stood.

"Ha! I have no weakness," Henrik chuckles.

"You have many, Henrik. Too many sometimes..."

"And what is your weakness, oh great Sigvard?" Finn asks with a devilish smile on his face.

I leave the tent, not wanting to hear any more of their troll talk. Keeping them around may prove to be my true weakness, but if they have not figured it out by now, they never will. It's time to check on the princess and her servant.

I find her bent over and gripping the bars so tightly her knuckles are white. Her legs are trembling, and she is doing everything in her power not to fall to her knees. A brief moment of dread passes over me, but I quickly push it aside. Her servant is yelling and flailing her arms in an attempt to get someone's attention.

"What seems to be the trouble, Princess?" I stroll over.

"Nothing." She does not even look at me.

"It doesn't appear to be nothing."

"Leave me the fuck alone, Sigvard. I am in no mood."

Her voice is soft and shaking, but I can tell she meant every word. I reach out and touch her hand, but the moment our skin makes contact, she pulls away. As she falls back onto the dirt, I observe her eyes are completely white.

She crashes into the dirt, her body completely limp and she remains motionless. Perhaps the gods have done me a favor and I don't need to kill her. I turn to leave when I hear the servant screaming.

"You can't just leave her to die! What kind of leader are you?"

I walk the distance to her cage. She is covered in sweat, tears, and dirt. "What is your name again?"

"Thyra. My name is Thyra."

"Thyra, do you want to know what I did to the people who kept me enslaved?" I pause only to take a breath, not wanting her to truly answer the question. "I killed them and not quickly. I let the torture last as long as the blood would flow."

Tears stream down her face, leaving trails in the layer of dirt that covers her.

"So, tell me, Thyra, why do you weep for the person who enslaved you?"

"Because Brynja did not enslave me. She. Set. Me. Free!"

Her words surprise me. No one can overhear her. There is no punishment awaiting her for telling the truth.

"And you know what else?" She pauses, but in turn does not wait for my answer. "She has absorbed more torture, more punishment than I, and still endures. So, please, do not let her die on this pissed-covered dirt for nothing!"

I want to question her. To know what she deems torture and punishment, but the glimmer of pain in her eyes stops me. I grit my teeth and return to the princess. She has not moved and her breathing appears shallow. I unlock the door and approach her slowly, my hand hovering over the hilt of my sword. As I kneel beside her, I realize how serious her condition is. I scoop her up into my arms and run to the lach.

The lach immediately removes me from his tent, and I pace outside, waiting for word of her condition. I have almost dug a trench into the dirt when Sten halts me.

"Brother, relax. The gods can feel your tension."

"I must know, but he won't let me in!" I scream at the tent.

"Why the sudden worry over the princess? You just told me this morning she was going to Niflheim. It appears Hel has handled it for you." He crosses his arms, a curl of amusement ghosts his mouth.

"And you will find yourself there with her if you do not shut your mouth."

He throws up his hands. "Apologies, Sigvard, I am just bemused by your sudden change of heart."

"I have no heart."

If I wasn't already displeased, Sten would have achieved it. Eternally challenging my motives. If we had not spent years chained together, I would question his loyalty. He moves closer and claps a hand on my shoulder.

"I know you do not like me defying you, but it is not truly defiance. It is offering guidance. You must know I stand with you until I am called to Valhalla?"

I sigh and clasp my hand on his opposite shoulder. "Of course, brother." He departs my presence until I call his name. He turns back around to face me. "What did she tell you to get you to come to me?"

"That is for her to tell you, if you are willing to listen."

My frustration finally overflows, and I charge into the tent only to find it empty. Where in the fuck did they go, and how did I not see them? The flap on the back side of the tent flutters in the breeze and I run out of it.

I find the lach, the princess, and Thyra at the lake. A large pestle and mortar sits on the edge of the shoreline. The lach and Thyra are on either side of the princess in the water. Thyra is dipping her hand into the water and repeatedly pouring the liquid over the princess's forehead while the lach says a prayer. I barrel into the water, unable to stop myself. It is as if someone were pushing me.

"Are you here to help or hinder, Sigvard?" the lach asks, the water sloshing around him from my entrance.

"Help. I want to help."

"Good. You hold her head. Thyra, you hold on tight to her hand... and mine."

·

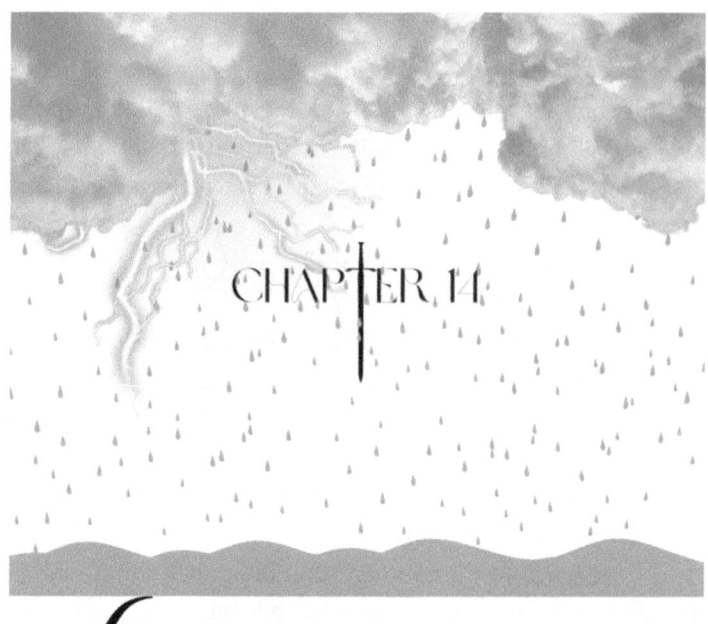

CHAPTER 14

Voices encircle me, but I'm lost in blackness. I'm trying to isolate voices to see if I can recognize something, anything, but it's chaos. I feel like I am getting too much air and not enough at the same time. Is this what death feels like?

Espen. Mother.

I say their names in my head, holding on to any sort of hope that I am not alone lost in this abyss when I hear five words.

"You are not finished yet."

I'm catapulted into the light and my lungs gasp in air like a newborn babe, and then I am underwater. What the fuck? Arms wrap around me and just as quickly as I sank, I am back above the water.

I cough hard as a hand rubs and pats my back. Between the black abyss and sudden submerging, my lungs feel like stone.

"Easy. Just breathe."

I take a few breaths until everything slows down before opening my eyes. Sigvard is holding me. Fuck. I must be dead. He couldn't have at least started off looking like Espen and then melted into Sigvard. I thought Hel would be more creative than this.

"Do you think you can stand?"

At least he is nice here.

"I'm not sure. Shouldn't I be stronger in the afterlife?"

He laughs and even his laugh is nice. Perhaps Loki is disguised as Sigvard. Do they have wine here? I'm going to need it.

"Princess, you are not dead. You were close, but Hel was not ready to take your soul."

"Doesn't help that Sigvard dunked you," Thyra says in the distance. I search for her and spot her standing on the shoreline with an older-looking gentleman.

"I didn't fucking mean to. She shot up like a dick in a whorehouse."

There he is. Fucking brute. I put my hand on his chest to get out of his arms and visions flash before me. Sigvard, covered in blood and screaming. A scream I am all too familiar with. One of absolute and total devastation. It is the same vision I had when he touched my hand on the cage. How did we go from the cage to the lake? I shake my head to clear the vision and the cobwebs from the last I-don't-even-know-how-many hours.

"Please put me down."

"As you wish." And he drops me into the water.

"Come on, Sigvard, she almost died. Can you not be an arse for two seconds?" Thyra says, annoyance heavy in every word.

"I held her heavy arse. I would consider that nice."

"Are you calling her fat?"

I lean back into the water and let myself float away from the never-ending chaos that seems to follow me. They can argue, I'm too exhausted to care. Just when I'm thinking I am far enough away, I feel someone next to me. Fortunately, it is Thyra.

"Are you alright?"

"Define alright."

I can see her smile out of the corner of my eye.

"Well, I am glad you are here."

"Agreed." I reach my hand for hers and she clasps it. We silently float, looking up at the colorful sky above us. The sun is starting its descent on the opposite side of the mountains, painting the sky with rose and gold. "What happened to me?"

"I think it was a mix of the heat and a vision, but I only told the lach I thought you were out in the heat too long."

Ah, so that older gentleman was a lach. It's all coming together except...

"How did you know I had a vision?" I do my best to look at her without losing my buoyancy.

"Your eyes went all white. Espen told me that happened before." Espen forever looking out for me. Did Sigvard observe this as well? Surely, he would have said something. "Come. Let's get dry and find some food."

I sit up and my long hair sticks to my back. "I doubt we will get any food, but I am ready to be dry."

"I have one of your favorite furs in my bag."

I suppose Espen isn't the only one always looking out for me. "That sounds wonderful."

Back in the camp, it's as if we don't exist. No resistance but no welcome either. Our bags were left by the cages, but our weapons are still unaccounted for. We decide to go to the far side of the camp and start a small fire. I take two branches and drive them into the dirt. A third branch is placed on top so we can lay our clothes on it to dry.

I sit on the fur I packed and wrap the one Thyra brought for me around my shoulders. I feel slightly refreshed but still need nourishment.

Thyra sits beside me in a tunic far too large for her. Her hair is down, encircling her shoulders, and she looks beautiful in the glow of the fire. Then it hits me.

"Is that Espen's tunic?"

She looks at me, the fire still twinkling in her eyes. "Yes."

We scootch closer together and let the memory of Espen warm us to the core. I swear I could fall asleep when I hear a voice.

"You ladies hungry?"

Sten is standing on the edge of the camp with a bowl in each hand. Once we both acknowledge his presence, he strides over. He hands Thyra a bowl first, and when I reach up for mine, the fur slides down my shoulders just enough to make it known I'm naked. Sten almost drops the bowl into my lap.

"Apologies, Princess, I didn't realize you were... that you weren't... you..."

"Naked, Sten? Yes, I am naked." I can't help but laugh as his cheeks flush a deep shade of red. "It's okay. I am properly covered, no need to apologize."

He leaves our small camp without another word.

"It seems your lack of clothing has left Sten with a lack of words."

"I would not have thought he would shy away from nakedness. I would have assumed he would welcome it."

"You are royalty, Princess," Thyra chides.

"If I could get everyone to stop calling me princess, that would be ideal." I wrap the fur tighter around me. I let it slide up to my nose to take in its smell. "I am so much... more than a princess. It's just a silly title and truly it means nothing."

"To some, title is everything because they assume it means freedom."

"If only they knew." I lean into her and close my eyes.

"If they only knew," she repeats, pressing back into me.

The next time my eyes open, the sun is peeking over the horizon. Thyra and I are now lying back-to-back. She is snoring softly, so I gently lay my fur over her and dash over to grab my clothes. They are dry and somewhat clean. Once dressed, I walk the outskirts of the camp. Even though I have only carried a blade for a short time, I feel bare without it. I hope it wasn't destroyed.

I wander into the forest near the mountain's edge where Magnus dropped us off. Sitting on a rock and looking deep into the woods is Sigvard.

"You are up early, Princess," he says without even turning to look at me.

"How did you know it was me?"

"Viking warriors are not known for being light on their feet. Henrik sounds like a maniacal wild boar."

I laugh. "And what do I sound like?"

He turns and looks at me. "A fox. I wouldn't have known of your presence if you hadn't stepped on that stick."

I climb up the rock and sit beside Sigvard. I didn't expect to see anything but trees from here, but the forest slopes, providing an unobstructed view of the valley below.

"You're only half-rotted today. Impressive."

Was that a compliment? "Thank you? Does this mean you will spare my life?"

"For now, but that doesn't mean you have earned my trust," he says, shifting the blade in his hand.

"How can I earn your trust?"

He looks at me, his eyes trailing every inch of me. There is nothing sexual or perverse about it, it's as if he is attempting to read me.

"You do understand my hesitation, don't you, Princess?"

"Stop fucking calling me that! I am so tired of it!" All the aggravation and disgust bubbles to the surface and erupts before I can halt it. I press two fingers between my eyebrows and take a deep breath. "Apologies Sigvard, but could you please call me Brynja?"

He nods, looking confused by my sudden outburst.

"Of course, I understand your hesitation but if you give me the chance, I can prove to you I am here for the right reasons," I say, crossing my arms.

"She can join me on guard duty tonight," a voice says from behind us.

Sigvard laughs. "Putting our lives into her hands is not an ideal way to test her loyalty, Sten."

"She will not be alone. She will be with me."

"And what happens when she kills you?" Sigvard glares at Sten.

"She will not."

I can feel his eyes on me, so I turn to meet his gaze, wondering how one line would make him so certain about me. I could be lying.

"If you wish," Sigvard says, standing and putting his blade back into the scabbard. "Just make sure to holler loud enough when she kills you so the rest of us don't perish."

Sigvard disappears into the woods, leaving Sten and me alone.

We stand silently, looking in the direction Sigvard headed. I have no words as no one has ever just trusted me. Except Espen. The king never did. Even as a child, he was always sure I had negative intent. When I was five, one of his rings went missing. He was convinced I took it. No matter how much I cried and swore on my life it wasn't me, there was no persuading him.

His words rang in my memory. *You are always playing dress-up. You took it so you could pretend to be the queen you will never be.*

Those words crawled deep beneath my skin and made a home there. Even after the ring was found among one of the servants' things, it didn't matter. I had to be entangled in it. He never apologized.

I place myself in front of Sten and put my hands on either shoulder. "Sten. I don't know what I did to deserve your trust but, thank you."

He gives a smug look. "You can thank me by proving me right. Meet me here at sundown."

∼

"Are you sure this is a good idea?" Thyra asks as she escorts me to the rock even though I asked her not to at least a hundred times.

"Yes, I'm sure. Can you please relax? You are freaking me out."

"How can you help guard without your sword? What if someone attacks? What if y—"

"Thyra. Please." I cut her off before she goes down another rabbit hole.

As soon as the rock comes into view, so does Sten. Unlike when I met him, he wears a black tunic and chest protector. His hair is pulled up into a bun and he has both a sword and a bow slung over his back. Somehow, he looks sexier than he did shirtless and sweaty. I peel my eyes away from him and pull Thyra into my arms.

"Do not worry about me. I will be fine. Promise."

"How do you make promises that you don't know you can keep?"

I remove her from my embrace and hold her at arm's length. "I do know I can keep it. You just have to trust me."

She mulls it over before nodding and reluctantly walking away. I watch to make sure she doesn't turn back. It wouldn't be the first nor the last time Thyra kept a watchful yet cautious eye on me.

"Come Brynja. It will be dark soon," Sten calls out to me impatiently.

I join him on the rock, and he is smiling like a fool but not saying anything. I have no idea if he is attempting to flirt or to kill me.

"Out with it, Sten. You are disturbing me," I say, crossing my arms.

He continues to smile like a fool but hands me my sword and scabbard. I look at it in disbelief, not sure that it is real until it touches my hand. I slam myself into Sten's chest and hug him as hard as I can. He hesitates briefly before wrapping his arms around me in return. His hug is the perfect mix of strong and soft, reminding me it has been far too long since I received a proper hug. Thyra gives wonderful hugs, but there is just something different... comforting about being wrapped up in a man's arms.

I realize I have hung on far too long and remove myself from his grasp. I clear my throat, pull down my tunic, and place my sword at my back. The moment it is in place, I feel complete. Like a warrior.

Sten smiles at me. "Come. Let me show what the night has in store."

~

GUARD DUTY IS VERY SIMPLE, especially with the two of us. Sten has one corner, I have the other, and we rotate periodically to make sure we don't fall asleep. The first several hours were easy, but as it creeps closer to the early morning, my eyelids feel like stone. Sten gave me a cup of water and every so often, I take sips to keep myself alert. I'm prepared to take another sip when I hear a noise way off in the distance. My blood tingles and I look around to make sure it isn't Sten, but he is nowhere in sight.

I stand and slowly move toward the sound. The farther away I get from the camp, the more my blood tingles. I'm not sure what it means, but it has to mean something. Just when I think I should turn around, I hear two sticks crack followed by muffled voices. I freeze, listening carefully to the directions of the voices. They are moving north away from the camp but still too close for comfort.

Moving quietly, I position myself so I am behind them. Once close enough, it becomes clear who is wandering about. Six of the king's guards, based on their attire and colors. I have the jump on them, but I am still outnumbered six to one. Do I risk my life to save the whole camp?

You know what to do. Don't hesitate. Trust your blade. Trust yourself.

Espen's voice echoes in my head. I'm not sure if I am

hearing a memory or if he is speaking to me, but I trust him. He always protected me. Always guided me, even when I wasn't ready. Now is my time. I wanted to prove my worth and the gods have served me an opportunity. I press my fingers to the rune of protection painted on my cheek, and kiss Espen's necklace before rushing out of the brush with my sword held high.

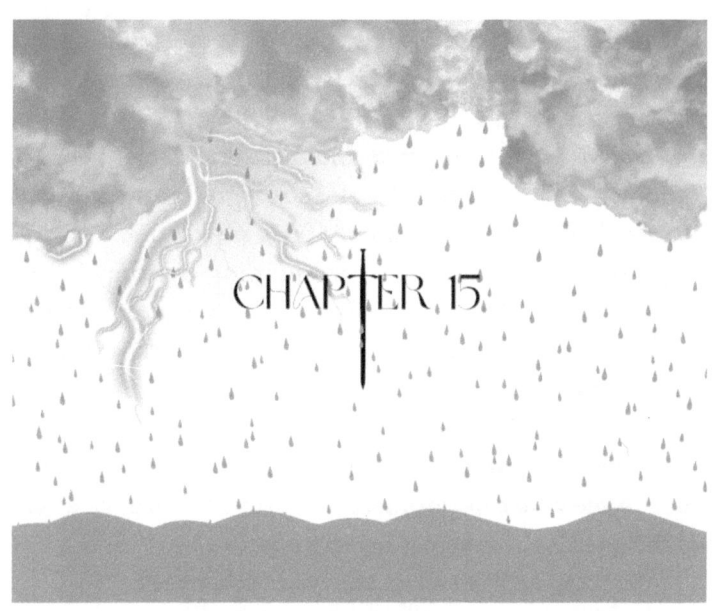

Chapter 15

The blade of my sword penetrates the nearest body with such ease I question briefly if I missed my mark. I pull it free and slice down on my next victim furiously. Hot blood splatters across my cheeks. Screams of pain and war reverberate around me, fueling my rage and eliminating any doubt. Two bodies down, four to go.

My presence is no longer a secret, but they are not properly organized. Surprise and fear dominate them. The third guard pulls his sword from his scabbard and lunges toward me, but his move is fatal. I glide my sword through his eye socket and back out before he hits the ground.

The remaining three attempt to surround me, but I know better. Espen taught me better. Our swords collide as I move around the guards. This requires them to exert more effort, trying to keep up or predict my next move. One decides to get daring and run toward me. I drop onto one knee and use my back and sword to catapult him up and over. Blood rains down on me as if Tyr, the God of War, is baptizing me.

I face the remaining two, and there is a moment of hesitation on their part. A look of fear, recognition, and disgust paints their features. This only fuels me further. I charge them both, a hearty battle cry unfurling from my blood-soaked lips. All three of our swords clang together and echo loudly against the mountainside. I slice, duck, dive, and stab at them relentlessly, taking blood each time. Their blades are not nearly as accurate.

I hear my name loudly from behind and, on instinct, turn to see who calls for me. Sten sprints toward me as one of the guards slices across my shoulder.

"Fucking hell!" I swear, annoyed with myself.

My fury rages as I stab the guard who just cut my shoulder twice in his gut just below his chest plate. He drops to one knee but continues to slice and jab in my direction. My sword clashes with the last man standing, and he smiles down on me with pleasure.

"I will kill you, Princess," he says, pressing his body weight into his sword.

"Only in your dreams." I roll away from him.

He falls flat onto his face, and before he can get up, I stab my sword through his back and into his heart. Blood pools out onto the dirt when I remove my sword. I turn back to the man on his knee. He has dropped his sword and is holding up his hands in defeat. I laugh and slice off his head.

Six down.

His body falls to the ground with a thud, and I wipe my sword off on my trousers before returning it to the scabbard. My chest heaves with exertion and sweat rolls down my back. I see Sten circling the ring of devastation out of the corner of my eye.

"You killed them all."

It sounds like a statement, but I presume he means it as a question. He is surprised by what he has witnessed.

"Yes. I did." I bend down to pick up the head of the guard. "Here, I assume Sigvard will want this."

"You should present it to him yourself."

I laugh. "For what purpose? Men like him only see what they wish. To him, I am nothing more than a helpless princess." I force the head into his hands.

"What I witnessed was far from helpless and I will tell him such." He turns the head over and grabs it by the hair.

"If you wish, but don't be surprised when he doesn't believe you," I say, attempting to brush the hair that is stuck in blood out of my face.

Sten places the head on the dirt and walks over to me. Gently, he removes the stuck hairs one by one before tucking them behind my ear. His fingertips trail down the edge of my neck and over to my chin. He grips it lightly and guides my eyes up to meet his.

"Only one of us is covered in blood."

ALL EYES ARE on me as we walk through camp toward Sigvard's tent. I think my appearance must be ghastly, but they are likely well acquainted with such sights. That is, until Thyra's eyes land on me.

"Brynja! You are hurt! We must get you to the lach."

"I am fine, Thyra, please calm your nerves." I take her hand in mine and do my best to soothe her.

"You certainly don't look fine." Before I can say another

word, we are in Sigvard's tent. Thyra keeps her mouth shut, but how her fingers twitch lets me know she is far from appeased.

Sigvard is all laughs and excitement until he sees me.

"If you were going to torture the princess, Sten, I wish you would have allowed all of us to play." His laugh and vindictive smile deepen.

"The blood she wears is not hers," Sten says very matter-of-factly.

A look of confusion laces Sigvard's features. "Then whose blood is it?"

Sten shifts to the side so I can step forward. I know my role, but I am all too aware this won't be received well. Reluctantly, I release Thyra's hand, untie the head from my bag, and place it on the table between Sigvard and myself.

His eyes bounce between the head, me, and Sten.

"What kind of hoax is this?" Sigvard asks, his eyes still moving between us.

"This is no hoax. Brynja ensured the safety of our camp." Sten spits in the dirt.

"She is covered in blood. Truthfully, I have no notion how she remains standing. Letting her take credit for your slaughter is quite bold."

I go to speak, but Sten steps in front of me, his hand resting lightly on my shoulder.

"Have I ever given you a reason to question me, Sigvard?" Before Sigvard can fully register the question, Sten continues. "The answer is I have not, and I witnessed with my own eyes Brynja slay not only this man"—he uses his other hand to point at the severed head—"but five others."

Sigvard laughs uncontrollably. "Sten, you must have fallen asleep and dreamed such nonsense. There is no way the princess could have taken on six grown men on her own. The king's guard is no match for us but for her..."

Sten holds my shoulder tighter, and if he didn't have a grip on me, I would have leaped across the table. It is one thing to be insulted but another to have it done directly in front of you.

"Stop fucking speaking about me like I am not present." I slam my hands onto the desk, causing the head to roll off and onto the floor. "If you truly think I am a liar, say it to my face."

Sigvard opens his mouth to speak but for some reason changes his mind. His eyes bore into me. "Go see the lach," is all he says.

I want to argue. Scream. Just shout out all the things that I have been holding in, but per usual I do as I am told. I do manage to storm off even though I have no idea where I am going.

"Brynja, wait!"

I manage to stop my forward momentum but not my eyes from rolling. "Sten, I'm not in the mood. Please, just leave me be." I don't turn around.

"You are going the wrong way..."

I stay in place, unwilling to move or say anything. Embarrassment and shame have been suffocating my life for far too long. I don't think I can handle anymore.

"Come, let me show you where the lach's tent is."

I face Sten. His eyes are filled with compassion, a world apart from how Sigvard looked at me moments ago. It's unfair for me to punish Sten when he did nothing wrong. All he has tried to do since I arrived is be amenable. Thyra is standing in his shadow and slowly mouths the word *please*. I nod and follow him.

The lach seems surprised by my appearance, which I

find rather odd. I am sure I am not the first bloody person to set foot in his tent. Perhaps I am the first bloody person still standing, but I doubt that as well. He circles me, taking in my full appearance before deciding what to do.

"We must get you in the bath so I can determine where you are bleeding from."

The humiliation continues. Now I must undress and bare all in front of a man I don't know. I don't even know his name.

"Ivar will not hurt you. You are in good hands, Brynja," Sten says from behind me.

I question how he knew my inner thoughts but quickly realize he was merely reading my body language. I am rigid and withdrawn.

"I will help prepare the bath," Thyra says quickly, grabbing a jug and exiting the tent.

"And I shall give you privacy."

I spin around. "Please don't go," I beg, our eyes meeting once more. "It would help to see another friendly face." I do my best to smile.

He smiles back. "If you wish me to stay, I will stay."

I study my reflection in the steamy water. A mix of memories with Mormor and the battle from this morning clash in my mind. Thyra rubs my shoulders, attempting to offer me comfort, but it is lost somewhere in the sea of emotions swarming my body.

"May I help you remove these blood-soaked clothes?" Her voice is gentle and kind.

"That would be wonderful," I say, still gazing at my reflection.

The rain of blood that fell upon my head turned my

sandy locks crimson. Thyra meticulously removes my gear and sets it aside. As she removes each piece, a similar weight is lifted from my inner being. Once I am down to my tunic and trousers, I insist on doing it myself.

Wet blood remains on my shoulder where the one guard wounded me. With my tunic removed, it trickles down my bare skin. It takes some effort to remove my trousers as they are stiff and hardened with dry blood. Thyra, Sten, and Ivar all move to help me, but I hold up my hand. This is difficult enough without three people trying to remove my trousers.

With the last bit of my dignity removed, I step into the hot water. Having just come off the fire, it is so hot it causes my skin to tingle, but it is a welcome feeling. I sink up to my neck, turning the water pink. Thyra moves to my side, but I sink below the surface, wishing to disappear if only for a moment.

The water envelops me, and I squeeze my eyes tightly, imagining it is Espen or my mother hugging me instead. As the air in my lungs decreases and I enter the gray area between life and death, I hear a voice.

"Oh, sis. When are you going to stop being so hard on yourself?"

"When you come back to life."

"I'm afraid that is not an option."

"I don't know what to do."

"Yes, you do. You just have to stop being afraid."

My body is pulled upward, and the moment I break the surface, my lungs gasp for air. Thyra pats my back and Sten pushes strands of wet hair out of my eyes.

"Brynja, what were you doing?" Thyra asks, confused.

"Espen."

Her pats turn to gentle rubs.

"Who is Espen?" Sten asks.

Thyra gazes at me, trying to read my thoughts before answering Sten. "Espen is Brynja's brother. What about him, sweet friend?"

"I... He... He was speaking to me."

The moment the words leave my mouth, I regret them. I know Thyra will believe me, she always does, but Sten and Ivar will question my sanity. I do not wish to be locked up anymore.

"Let me wash your hair. That will make you feel better." Thyra acts like I didn't say anything unusual.

While Thyra washes my hair, I scrub the rest of my body. I had no idea dried blood would be such an aggravation. Sten and Ivar speak quietly in the corner, Sten's eyes occasionally finding mine. I wish I could hear what they are discussing, but there is no doubt it involves me. It takes Thyra three washes to get all the blood out of my hair and the water has gone from pink to deep red as a result.

Ivar breaks away from Sten and walks over to the side of the wash container. He is wringing his hands over and over again.

"Apologies, Princess, but I am going to need you to stand. Just so I can see your injuries."

"Don't apologize to her. She brought this on herself," Sigvard says, entering the tent with no warning or care.

Both Thyra and Sten go to defend me, but I stand up out of the water with no hesitation. All their eyes are on me as the water saunters down my curves. Thyra covers her mouth in surprise, but I let pride wash over me instead of shame. My brother is right, I have to stop being afraid. They haven't even seen the real surprise yet. I take my time turning around, letting them get a long look at my back before facing them again.

"Have you gotten a good enough look?" I glare at Sigvard. He is visibly stunned. "Thyra, would you please get my fur?"

She darts out of the tent quickly to obtain my fur so I do not have to stand here in humiliation any longer. What she does not know or realize is I am not the one feeling uncomfortable. They are.

I step out of the water and sit in a nearby chair, legs crossed, waiting on Thyra's return. Ivar is the only one who is able to find his words.

"Let me bandage the wound on your shoulder, Princess. It does not appear deep enough to require cauterization."

"That would be most appreciated, Ivar, and please, call me Brynja."

He nods and grabs a small pot from the fire near the front of the tent before pulling up a chair beside me. He applies pressure to ensure the wound has stopped bleeding and then grabs the pot.

"This may hurt, but it will make certain the wound will heal."

I know exactly what he is doing as I saw Mormor do it many times. "I know it will. My mormor was a lach."

For the first time, I see his eyes soften and a smile pull across his lips. "Who was your mormor?" He uses the question to distract me as he pours the hot honey onto my shoulder.

"Alva Thorsson," I say, gritting my teeth together as the liquid begins cooling against my skin. He quickly begins wrapping a bandage around it.

"Lach Thorsson is a legend. Many believed she saved all of Thora from succumbing to smallpox. I was not aware you were related."

"Did you say Thora?" Sigvard asks, invading the conversation.

"Yes. He did," I say angrily. "If you had taken the time to find out anything about the king, aside from your hatred, you would know his wife, my mother, was from Thora." I stand up, closing the small space between us. "Which is why he killed her and my brother."

Chapter 16

- Sigvard

She is gone from sight before I even finish pondering her words. Thora. Her mother is... was from Thora? Meaning she too has Thoracian blood. And her back. What had done that to her back?

"Ivar, were those old wounds on her back?" I ask, unsure if my eyes were deceiving me.

"Indeed. They appear to be from years and years of torture."

I shudder as the words take me back to my years as a slave. There are still nights when I wake swearing I can hear the crack and feel the sting of a whip.

"Who would have tortured her so?" As far as I know, she has only been on the run for a few weeks now.

"The king." Thyra's words are so faint I almost miss them.

I turn and see her standing at the entrance to the tent holding the fur she went to fetch. "You are saying her father did this to her?"

She nods. A single tear slides down her cheek. "She tried to give you hints. There is a reason she does not call him Father."

"Fuck." I run a hand through my hair.

Sten claps a hand around my shoulder. "I tried to tell you as well, brother. You let your feelings cloud your judgment."

"Spare me your filth today."

I turn my attention back to Thyra, but she's gone—likely off to find the princess, who ran off half-clothed. And now I'm left to endure Sten's rot. It is clear she has opened up to him. I run a hand through my hair again and take a breath to prepare mentally for the verbal lashing Sten is sure to give.

"Tell me all you know," I say, making eye contact with him so he knows I am serious.

"That is all I know. Truly. Her... scars were unknown to me."

"But you knew of her mother and brother?"

"That is why I suggested you release her."

"And why did you not tell me yourself?"

"That is not my story to share, Sigvard. Don't be foolish."

He irritates the fuck out of me, but I can't argue his reasoning.

"Once she is dressed, ask her to come see me." I attempt to leave the tent, but Sten grabs my arm.

"You should go to her. I believe you have embarrassed her enough for one day."

Averse to give Sten complete satisfaction, I say, "I have a

few things I must tend to first. Then I will speak with her." I pull my arm from his grasp and leave before he can say another word.

Back in my tent, I can't focus on anything. Images of Brynja's back and naked body keep flashing through my mind. How did I not get word that the queen and the future king were slaughtered, and not only that, but felled by the king's hand? My scouts should have at least known of their demise. There must be a reason the king is keeping it close to the chest, which makes Brynja's story more credible. If it were known he killed his own family, there would be an uprising. The remaining question is why Brynja was spared.

"Henrik. Finn. Organize the men. I need you to go to Thora."

"Thora? What awaits in Thora?" Finn asks.

"Information. I need you to find out everything you can about the queen and her family."

"Who gives a fuck about the queen?" Henrik chides.

"And the king is going to have eyes on Thora. This could put us in danger," Finn adds, reminding me why I keep him around.

"I don't give a fuck. If we want to defeat the king, to make this rebellion worth the bloodshed, then we can't ignore what could collapse his entire empire."

"Don't tell me you believe the princess," Henrik says, continuing to give me hell.

"If I wanted lip, I'd whip out my dick. Do what I fucking ordered."

He goes to speak again like the dumb cock that he is, but Finn grabs him and removes him from my presence. If they return without the proper information, I will cut off Henrik's cock and shove it down Finn's throat.

When they return, a new location will be required. I do

not desire to move. We have everything we need here, including game to hunt and plenty of water. With the princess discovering us and the risk I am taking sending the men into Thora, it's only a matter of time. I stand over the map, scanning for a place. Nothing jumps out at me. I prefer to be far enough away that it's a pain in the arse for the king's army, but my men still can spy and observe. Being on the run for this long, our choices are becoming limited.

Perhaps I could extend our watch perimeter instead. Only one side is vulnerable. No one will come directly over the mountains, too taxing. Same with the lake.

"Sigvard!" Thyra yells before storming into my tent. "Where is she?"

"Where is who?"

"Don't play stupid with me. Where is Brynja? What have you done with her?" She attempts to grab me, but Sten wraps his arms around her.

"What are you talking about? I have not seen her since she stormed out of Ivar's tent naked." I stab my knife into the map on the table.

"Don't fucking lie to me. Where. Is. She!" Her voice escalates with each word and shatters on "she" as she collapses onto the ground. I pity this woman, so deeply attached to someone she was forced to serve. Sten is beside her, trying to comfort her. His display of softness makes me turn away.

"I am not lying. I have not seen or spoken to the princess."

"Then where could she be?" Thyra asks, her voice shaky and barely audible.

I did not plan to spend my day looking for a rogue princess, but I cannot have a distraught woman on my hands, either. I pull the knife out of the map and stick it back in my belt.

"Come. Let us look."

"We already did. We looked everywhere," Thyra whines at me. I grunt in disgust.

"Did you barge into my tent just to be infuriating, or do you want my help?"

I am astonished Sten has not spoken. He is not one to keep his opinions quiet, yet the time he chooses to be silent is the time I wish he would not.

Thyra returns to her feet. Her face is smudged with dirt and tears. She attempts to wipe it away with her sleeve, but it only makes it worse. The moisture in her eyes catches the sunlight illuminating them. Sea green... just like my...I shake my head, clearing the thought.

"If you just wish to be infuriating, leave," I say, turning away from them.

"No. Please. I am just... worried." She rounds the table and places her hand on my shoulder. "Your help would be much appreciated."

Without making eye contact, I exit the tent to look for the princess.

AFTER AN EXCESSIVE NUMBER OF LAPS, Thyra is utterly panicked and there is no sign of the princess. She retrieved her gear from Ivar's tent but managed to do so unseen. We asked every person we encountered if they saw her, but no one had.

"Any thoughts on where she would go?" I ask Sten, who has been chillingly quiet.

"No, particularly alone."

"Gather two others and see if you can trail her."

Sten stops and looks at me. "First you want to kill her and now you want to find her. Which is it, Sigvard?"

"Do you want to find the princess or argue my faults?" I struggle to keep my voice under control.

He bites his lower lip and looks away before nodding and walking off. I will have to swallow my pride and admit fault, not only to him but to the princess. To do that, we have to find her first. Before someone else does.

Chapter 17

Taking off alone is foolish but, I'm just so weary of being in places I am not truly wanted. I'd rather die among the trees fighting for myself than shoulder-to-shoulder with those who don't trust me. Even after I bared all to Sigvard, and my loyalty remained in question. I'm not sure who is worse, him or the king.

I began this journey looking for a seer. For answers. That is where my focus will remain. The small town of Alpta sits at the base of Fellheim, opposite the side Thyra and I took to get to Sigvard. Mormor told me many stories of Alpta. Its unique beauty calls seers to visit for enlightenment and to connect to the Goddess of the Earth, Jord. It will be the perfect place to find temporary solace and the answers I desire.

Fellheim, though a range of mountains, is not as elevated to the north. Rivers run through the rocks, eroding their possibility of reaching great heights. A large forest encircles the area, the same forest where I slaughtered the six men. It is the simplest route to get to and from Sigvard and his camp, which is why they keep eyes on it, but it is not without its challenges. Giant slopes and deep chasms appear out of nowhere, ready to take an unsuspecting victim.

I do my best to keep a steady pace, but not so quickly that I end up paying the price. I learned my lesson. Thyra can't find me—I would not be able to turn her away. She may not believe it, but I left her for her benefit. She does not need to be constantly in danger due to my presence.

I stop beneath a tree to take a breath and eat a few bites of food. A river roars like a lion to my right, while off to my left, it is peacefully silent. The breeze gently tickles my neck, and I feel a semblance of peace for the first time in a long time. I wish I could share it with my mother and Espen.

A branch snaps nearby, and I'm on my feet immediately. I move toward the river, hoping to find a hiding place among the rocks. Running would be too risky. I had questioned if anyone would attempt to follow me. There is a chance it could be an animal, but my gut tells me it is not.

I slide behind a collection of rocks near the water's edge and close my eyes. If I can't see them, they can't see me, right? Hopefully, they will pass by, and I can be on my way. I want to get as close to Alpta as I can before dark. Sleeping in the woods would not bother me with Thyra. We could rotate shifts, one always keeping watch while the other slept. I am much more vulnerable alone.

Someone splashes the water in anger, and I hold my breath.

"Sigvard is going to have my fucking balls."

I know that voice. I peek my head up and see the walking temptation himself. Sten. I slide back out of sight and debate for a moment if I want to acknowledge his presence. He did come looking for me, but was it because he was ordered or because he cares?

"I could deliver your balls to him for you," I say. An unexpected smile forms on my face as I await his response.

"I'm not sure who would enjoy that more, you or him." His voice shifts into a playful tone.

He stalks closer, following my voice, but the rocky sand gives him away despite how slow he moves. As he circles closer, I climb up the rocks.

"What are you doing out here, Princess? Thyra is distraught."

Look at him playing on my emotions. He is preparing to surprise me around the corner where I was initially hiding, but unfortunately for him, he is the one who will be surprised.

I jump off the rock and make direct contact with Sten. In my mind, I wrapped my body around him like a spider monkey, and he struggled to fight me off. In reality, we both end up face-first in the sand.

"What in Hel's name, Brynja?" Sten moans, rolling onto his back.

I flop onto my back and look over at him. He moans and groans for a moment longer before his eyes find mine. After several breaths, we burst out laughing. I had forgotten how good it feels to laugh.

"That did not go according to plan," I say once the laughter in my chest settles.

"There was a plan? Was the intended outcome my death?"

"You truly think I would kill you? You are the only one who believes me."

"No, but I don't believe you had a plan. Who catapults themselves at someone?" He rises to his feet, brushes off some of the sand, and offers me his hand.

"I didn't say it was a good plan, although it played out well in my head." I take his hand. His grip is firm and riddled with calluses, but it somehow has a softness. I believe there is much more to Sten than his demanding exterior presence. I also suspect the same thing of Sigvard; the difference is, Sigvard is an arsehole.

Sten smirks. "Did you at least know where you are headed, or were you just desperate to leave?"

"I know where I am headed and will continue to do so alone. Speaking of being alone, does Sigvard know of your intentions?"

My curiosity is piqued. There is no way Sigvard would have sent him after me alone. No one from that camp travels alone, nor should they.

"He does not. I was sent to find you with two others, but I deserted them." His smirk widens.

Now I am really curious. Why would he abandon two of his allies to find me alone? I am no one to him.

"Why?"

"It breaks me to see Thyra so devastated, and if I keep pissing off Sigvard, he will send me to Valhalla."

"Sigvard would be a damn fool to kill you," I say, unable to stop myself from grinning at him.

"I'm pleased to hear you think so. Now tell me, where are we traveling to?"

He brushes off the remaining sand. This is the first time I have seen him in full battle gear. Much like Booth, the gear does not hide the appeal of his body.

His muscles test the confines of his tunic each time he moves, and his long hair is pulled up high on his head.

As much as I would love his company, he really can't stay with me. I imagine that would only make his situation with Sigvard worse. He left everyone behind for me. Why would he risk it?

"Sten, I appreciate your... protectiveness, but I will be fine. You should return to camp." I turn away from him, knowing if I gaze upon him much longer, I will not be able to say no.

"I am not leaving. If I must follow you like a dog, then so be it."

No additional words are said. I continue on my way to Alpta, and Sten follows closely behind.

As the day transforms into night, the air chills, and the smell of rain hangs heavy in the air. In my haste to leave the castle, I did not bring much to protect me from the rain besides the furs. The skin sides of all furs are treated with animal fat to repel rain and still provide warmth. If a heavy rain occurs, my two furs will be no match. Especially all evening.

"Brynja, I suggest we halt our progress until morning. Freyr and Thor are devising a storm we should not be caught in."

How did he know what I was thinking?

"Alpta is not much farther; perhaps we can make it."

He stops and crosses his arms. "Not even a wolf can outrun a determined god. Don't be foolish. I have packed shelter."

It is my turn to cross my arms. "You planned to shelter with me?"

"Don't be daft, Princess. I don't control the gods. A smart warrior carries what is required to survive." He removes the pack from his back.

"Don't call me princess. Are you saying I am not a smart warrior?" My displeasure rises.

"At this moment, you are being an emotional warrior."

"Ha!" I laugh in annoyance and walk off. He is in front of me before I can take ten steps.

"Brynja," he says, gently wrapping a hand around my shoulder. "I meant no disrespect, but a storm is coming, and we do not have time to quarrel."

A part of me wants to continue arguing with him, but he is right. I don't have to tell him he is, though.

Silently, we work together to put up a small tent. The wind threatens to blow us and the tent away, but we fight against it and get underneath before Thor rips the sky apart. The inside of the tent is just large enough for us both to lie side by side. I place my more extensive fur on the ground and my sword beside it. Usually, I would strip down, but not with Sten present. I choose to stay as I am and use my other fur as a pillow instead of a blanket.

I close my eyes and prepare to fall into another world. As I start to forget the chaos going on outside and drift, Sten is creating chaos inside. I open an eye and see him stripping off his tunic. I fight the urge to open the other eye and instead roll onto my side so my back is to him. Removing him from sight only seems to amplify my hearing. I can clearly make out every movement he makes as if I could see it.

· · ·

His belt sliding off his waist.

The cloth sliding over his thighs.

His hair falling to his shoulders.

I fight the urge to move a single muscle, wanting him to assume I am asleep. Once he lies down, I can drift off and be anywhere I want. I just need him to stop stripping.

I feel his weight beside me and quietly thank the gods I survived. I pull my knees in and snuggle into the furs. Perhaps I can find my mother tonight in my dreams. I have encountered Espen in numerous ways, but not her. Not once.

A heavy arm drapes over me, and I am instantly surrounded by his heat.

"You look cold. Let me warm you."

I want to believe he is a gentleman, as Sten has been courteous to me since our first encounter. It's just the lack of clothing has me leaning toward other motives.

"Sten. You might want to try a more gracious approach in your seduction techniques."

He laughs deeply from his chest. I turn over, ready to give him a tongue lashing, when I see his naked body only partially covered by his fur. Every word that was in my head vacates immediately. He smiles up at me, one hand behind his head.

"Trust me, if I were trying to seduce you, you would not still have on all your clothes. I can't comprehend why you do now. Do you always sleep fully clothed?"

"No."

"Then why are you? You weren't shy with your nudity before." His smile widens.

"You saw me at the fire? Is that why you ran away?" I ask, well aware I am blushing.

"I did not, but it felt... inappropriate. I may be a brute, but that doesn't mean I don't have manners. Not all of us are like Sigvard. We had a life before all of this. Truthfully, so did he."

Sten's entire mood has shifted. The smile that brightened his face has vanished, and he is lost in the dark memories of the past. I had let myself forget that these men are just that—men. Sten gave up his entire life for his family. Not just any man would do that.

"Apologies, Sten, that was... inappropriate of me."

"None needed, Brynja. I believe we understand each other more than either of us realize." He smiles again, but it is much more forced than his previous smile. "Will you at least remove your battle gear? It can't be comfortable."

I nod and slide off the metal bracer cuffs that Booth made for me. As I remove the leather bracer, Sten takes my arm. "May I?"

"Sure."

He leisurely unties each bracer, slides them off my wrists, and places them to the side. He motions for me to give him my legs, and I oblige. His large, warm hand cups the back of my thigh as he works to remove both leg wraps. Once they are removed, he twirls his finger in the air to tell me to turn around. We exchange grins, and I turn so my back faces him.

He loosens my chest plate. His hot breath trails down my neck and collects at the swell of my breasts. The scent of his skin washes over me, a concoction of pine, mint, and seawater. Not at all what I expected. His hands wrap around the tops of my arms and guide them up into the air. Simultaneously, we rise on our knees as he slides my chest plate off. His nose presses against my ear as my chest plate falls to the earth.

He lingers, just taking me in. Our bodies pressed together, I let my head fall back on his chest. His fingers trail through my hair, and I let the comfort take over, leaving me with no strength to move. He barely grazes my ear with his lips as he moves down my neck to my collarbone. His hands wrap around my thighs, his fingers digging into my skin. Our heads turn, and he raises his so we are at eye level. Our lips are now mere inches apart. He moves closer. Only a molecule of air separates us. My whole being fills with waiting. Wanting.

"We should sleep," he says, releasing me, breaking the magnetism that was quickly building.

"Of course." I try to sound poised.

I curl onto my side, exhaustion finally settling into my bones. With a whispered prayer to the gods, I surrender to sleep.

When I wake, the air is cool and still. The tent is dim, washed in the muted blue of early dawn.

Sten is gone.

He must have slipped away the moment sunlight brushed the horizon. I can't say I'm surprised—but something feels off.

His clothes are still here. Folded. Undisturbed in the corner.

Where would he have gone... without them?

I exit the tent and scan the area. Leaves and branches scatter the forest floor from last night's storm, but there is no sign of Sten. I turn back to the tent to gather my things when I hear water splashing. Walking the short distance back to the river, I look around for the source. The water rushes by. Perhaps I was just hearing it against the rocks, but when I hear it again, I know without question that it is man-made.

Rounding the corner, past the stack of rocks I hid behind, I come to a calm area of the river. Blocked off by a dam, a perfect pool of water sits undisturbed—except for Sten. He stands in the middle of the pool, back toward me, scrubbing his arms. The tattoo I had glimpsed previously was just a sneak preview. His entire back is a masterpiece. The tree of Yggdrasil is centered on his mid-back. Around it are displays of war, but the image that grabs my attention the most is of the dragon perched on his shoulder blade.

Silently, I strip off my clothes and walk into the water. If he knows of my presence, he gives no indication until I touch his back. He stills beneath my fingers, and I trace the outlines of his tattoos with my fingertips. I am aware that encroaching on his space like this is bizarre, but I just couldn't help myself. It's as if I had to prove to myself that it was real.

"I am typically greeted properly before being propositioned," Sten says with a smile in his voice.

"Don't flatter yourself." I try to push whatever happened last night out of my mind and focus on the details of his tattoo.

He chuckles softly and turns to me, taking away my distraction. He is exquisite. His smile morphs him from a hardened warrior to a kindhearted man. That is, until he notices my nudity. He turns around and goes back to scrubbing his body.

"Brynja, I didn't mean to... I'm..." His words trail off, and he gives up trying to come up with something. This is twice now he has shied away from me, except last night. I cannot determine his purpose, but I am thankful for his kindness.

"No apologies are needed, Sten. I invaded your space. I will prepare our bags while you finish."

I exit the water before he can say another word.

I place his attire on the rocks near the water for him to find easily while I pack up the rest of the camp. Alpta is not much farther; we should be able to make it easily before dusk. Once I have everything in its place, I tend to my hair. It hasn't been brushed out properly in too long. My braid is a disheveled mess. I undo it and brush through my tangled locks until they are smooth.

Separating my hair into two sections, I braid each side, looping in blue ribbons that were once my mother's. She used them to tighten her favorite corset. I was never a fan of corsets. Too uncomfortable, but before my mother, the ribbons belonged to Mormor. She also used them for her hair. One as a headband to keep her hair out of her eyes. The other she used to tie up her braids. She never liked having hair on her neck.

"Brynja?" Sten kneels before me. "Are you alright?"

"Oh! Yes. I was just... thinking about my mother and Mormor."

"I can't imagine the emptiness you feel without them," he says, offering me a hand.

"Sure, you can. You have been without your family for three years."

"True, but I still have hope that they live."

I smile. "That is true."

"Shall we?"

I nod, and we walk together down the path toward Alpta. I envisioned myself on this trek many times before leaving Sigvard's camp. None of those included Sten by my side.

When we arrive in Alpta, the sun is still high in the sky, but my excitement quickly diminishes. What was once the town of Alpta, known for its unmatched ethereal beauty, is now nothing more than blood and ash.

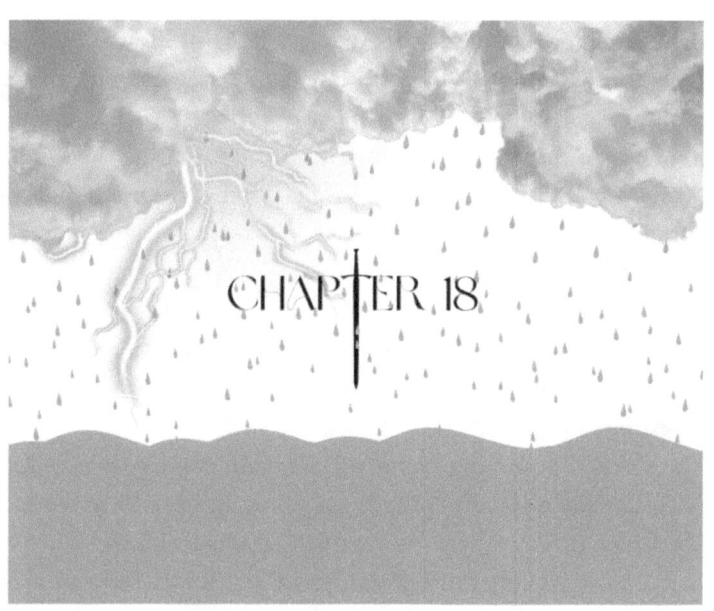

Chapter 18

The heat from the fire still lingers, and the smell of blood, sulfur, and burning flesh hangs heavy in the air. I call out, hoping someone will answer, but my calls are met with silence. A blonde-haired woman is lying on her side. She appears untouched by the destruction until I get closer. The front half of her body is completely charred. One arm reaches toward her home that no longer exists.

I kneel before her and tuck a strand of hair behind her ear. I pull the small knife from my boot to place it in her hand, but the moment our skin touches, I crash into a vision.

Fire roars around me. The heat is so intense that sweat immediately pours down my face. Screams and panic fill the air, making it impossible to breathe. The woman is now standing in front of me. She has a small child in one arm while her other arm reaches for another.

Their fingers are about to touch when the house behind the child explodes. It blasts her backward and me to the present.

I gasp in air as the remnants of Alpta come back into view. Tears stream down my face as the woman's heartbreak vibrates through my bones.

"Brynja, are you alright?"

I can't see Sten through my tears, and words feel utterly impossible, so I propel myself into his arms. I envision knocking him over, but he catches me and wraps his arms securely around me.

"Breathe, darling, breathe." He pulls me closer into his chest while also wrapping his legs around me to make me feel even more secure. "You are safe. I swear it."

I close my eyes and focus on taking long, deep inhales followed by slow exhales. Each time, my heart slows a touch more.

"Good. Very good," Sten says, placing his large palm on my head and holding me close so I can hear his heartbeat. It is slow and methodical yet strong, providing the last touch of calmness I need.

I press my face into his chest. "Thank you."

"It is no trouble, Brynja, but what sent you into such a state?"

"You wouldn't believe me if I told you."

"Lay it on me."

I remove myself from his grasp and sit across from him. His freckled eyes are filled with concern. I have never told anyone outside of my family about my visions. I am unsure how this will be received, but Sten deserves to know.

"I... have visions," I say, anxiously rubbing my thumbs together.

"What do you mean by visions?"

"When I touch people, I see things. Things that have happened to them."

"What do you see when you touch me?" He leans in, intrigued.

"That is the interesting part. It doesn't happen when I touch everyone, just certain people."

"And it occurred when you touched this woman?"

I shift uncomfortably, looking down at my hands before meeting his eyes again. "Yes. I saw her death."

"No wonder you were so shattered." He shifts his position so that one leg is straight and the other is bent. All I can do is nod as the vision replays in my mind. "Does this only occur when you touch the slain?"

"No. I had a vision when I touched Sigvard."

Sten's eyebrow raises with intrigue. "Truly? What did you see?"

I straighten my leg so my foot is touching Sten's. "He was covered in blood with a head in each hand."

He throws back his head and roars with laughter. "That is a daily occurrence for Sigvard."

I roll my eyes and stand up, brushing the dirt and ash off myself.

Sten jumps to his feet. "I didn't mean offense."

"You did not offend me, Sten. I do not doubt it is a regular occurrence for Sigvard." I walk through the rest of the debris, still hanging on to hope that we will find someone alive in the complete destruction surrounding us. "Do you believe me?"

"Absolutely, I do."

The fact that he doesn't question my visions warms my heart. I wouldn't blame him if he didn't; it sounds absurd.

"Have you ever considered that you might be a seer?" he asks, moving a pile of burnt wood.

The thought had not crossed my mind previously, but Mormor was a seer. Could it be possible?

"Seers see the future. I don't believe I am seeing the future but more the past."

"Or perhaps it just feels that way."

I have not thought much about how or why I get these visions. They started as vivid dreams, something I thought my imagination concocted until they started occurring with touch. Once I lost Espen and my mother, all my focus turned to finding Sigvard and joining the rebellion. It seems that each time I turn back to myself, something terrible happens.

"I had come here to talk to a seer. Hoping for some sort of answer, but it seems the gods have other plans for me."

Sten prepares to speak when a crashing noise comes from the far side of the destroyed town. My initial thought is just a building giving way, but the hairs on the back of my next stand up. Someone else is here.

"Who's there? Speak now or meet the end of my blade." I reach back, ready to pull my sword from its scabbard.

"Brynja, do you truly think it's smar—"

"Brynja?" calls another voice, shocking Sten and halting him mid-sentence.

I would think I was hallucinating if Sten didn't hear it as well. "Astrid?"

She walks into view mere steps away from me. Without another moment's hesitation, I run toward her. We collide into each other, wrapping our arms in a full embrace.

"I didn't think we would ever find you!" She squeezes me even tighter.

"I would have never thought you would come looking for me."

She pulls back and looks me up and down. "Of course

we would. I can't believe you left without us. Not even a word. I should be furious with you, but I am too delighted to have found you!"

"Where is your ill-tempered, flirtatious brother?" I smile back at her.

"Among the ruins, praying he doesn't find your body. He cannot fathom the possibility of you being gone before finally accepting his advances." She giggles. Always the shameless flirt. It does bring me joy to know he cared enough to look for me, even if his intentions are... humorous.

"Aksel! Come see what I have found!" Astrid yells out.

There is a loud ruckus; a bunch of stuff falls and scatters all over the ground before Aksel appears. He stares at me. His face has no emotion, so I wave at him like a fool.

"Sister, am I seeing things, or is that Princess Brynja in the flesh?"

"Why don't you walk over and find out for yourself?" A smirk pulls at the corners of her mouth.

Aksel walks over and stops directly in front of me. He slowly scans every inch of me, as if making sure I am not a figment of his imagination, some trick created by Loki. When he reaches my eyes, he stares for a long moment before pulling me into his arms.

"I would know those eyes anywhere. So good to see you!"

It doesn't take but a moment for his hands to trail toward my arse. He gives it a good squeeze; all I can do is laugh. I am accustomed to Aksel's mannerisms. Sten is not, and I can feel his presence as he steps closer, but he is not the only one.

Agnarr comes into my sight over Aksel's shoulder.

His braided hair has remnants of dirt and blood. The

scruff on his face has grown into a beard, and he is wearing a tight green tunic. The tension in his jaw betrays deep frustration, but his eyes, those deep blue eyes, contain waves of relief.

I release Aksel and walk the distance to Agnarr. I understand his frustration and anger. It is my fault that the last words my brother and he spoke to each other were unfavorable, and it cannot be undone. Yet he put his feelings aside to join the twins in looking for me.

"I thought I'd never see you again," I say, speaking truthfully.

"Neither did I. Once Orn told us you left, I was sure the king killed you."

"How is Orn? Please tell me he still lives?"

Agnarr nods and looks away as if looking at me is too painful to bear.

I go to speak again, but Sten beats me to it. "Are you going to introduce me to all of your friends?"

Agnarr's eyes dart in Sten's direction. A muscle flickers angrily in his jaw. I remain with Agnarr as I hear Sten, Astrid, and Aksel exchange pleasantries behind me. His hands clench stiffly at his sides while his eyes remain locked on Sten.

"Where did you acquire this brute?" He unclenches and clenches his hands.

I know the moment I say it, he'll come undone, but lying serves no purpose. "He is one of Sigvard's men."

"And why, pray tell, are you running around with one of Sigvard's men? Did you two run off to be together?"

I bite my tongue to contain my aggravation. He is angry with me and just lashing out. "It is not like that, Agnarr. I left Sigvard's camp when I was not deemed worthy to be there, and Sten came after me, knowing how dangerous it would be for me to travel alone."

"But why would one of Sigvard's men side with you, not him? That does not make sense, Princess."

"Then ask him yourself since my answers do not satisfy you."

He moves past me to Sten. The two exchange curious looks before Agnarr begins antagonizing him.

"Why would you abandon Sigvard to follow the princess?" he asks.

"I did not abandon anyone. Brynja did not deserve the treatment she received, nor should she be traveling alone. If any unfriendly eyes land up her, she will surely be killed."

"She is with friends now. You can see yourself back to where you belong." Agnarr presses his chest into Sten's. Sten is larger than Agnarr, but this does not faze him at all.

"I stopped taking orders long ago. The only way I will leave is if Brynja asks me to." Sten pushes back against Agnarr.

Both sets of eyes land on me. Blood pounds at my temples as my face grows hot with humiliation. I clear my throat to speak, but it is tight, as if someone is squeezing it.

"Princess, tell him that his services are no longer needed and that he should crawl back to his master."

Agnarr's attempt at stirring the pot works as Sten's blade finds his throat.

"Do not speak to me as if I am still a slave," he says, pressing the blade hard against Agnarr's skin.

Before I can protest, Sten's blade flies out of his hand. Aksel catches it with ease and rams it into the dirt.

"Everyone take a breath," he says, leaning on the sword.

"What in the Odin's arse just happened?" Sten asks, mystified.

"I took your sword." Aksel smirks, pulling the sword out of the ground, tossing it in the air, and catching it perfectly by the hilt.

"How did you do that?" I walk around Aksel like I might uncover something to explain what had just occurred.

He smiles and says, "Magic."

My head feels like it's spinning when Astrid touches my shoulder. "We've been wanting to tell you for years."

"Tell me what? That Aksel can cast spells or whatever that was," I say, moving my arms in circles.

"We are elves, Bryn." Did Astrid just say she and her brother are elves? How did I not know this? Or notice, for that matter. I fall onto my butt in the dirt. Astrid kneels beside me. "Bryn, are you alright?"

"I'm fine. I just... feel like a fool."

"Why don't we set up camp? We can stay here for the night, and I'll tell you everything," she says, cupping my chin tenderly. I find myself nodding without thought.

"Can I have my fucking sword back?" Sten asks, his voice hoarse with frustration.

Astrid and I smile at each other. "I like the brute," she whispers.

Aksel uses his powers to hurtle Sten's sword toward him. It sticks into the dirt between his feet. Sten removes the sword from the dirt and spins it in his hands a few times before returning it to his scabbard.

"I hate to confess this, but Aksel, that was badass," Sten says, smirking.

"I like the brute too. Don't tell Agnarr," Aksel whispers to us as he dashes by to go talk to Sten. Agnarr throws up his hands in defeat. It appears we will all be spending the evening together. I pray to the gods everyone can contain themselves.

We set up on the far side of the destroyed town, farthest from the road. Even though it is highly unlikely anyone would turn a second eye on an already ravaged town, it doesn't mean we should test our luck.

We do, however, make a small fire—just enough to provide some warmth and to cook the rabbits Sten caught for dinner. We sit around in awkward silence, no one wanting to be the first to speak.

"In the stories I was told as a child, elves always had pointy ears," Sten says, taking a hearty bite of his share of rabbit. I am just happy someone is speaking. I currently cannot find the words to express all the thoughts circling my mind.

"Common misconception," Aksel says. "We are actually sexy as fuck."

"Way to be humble, brother," Astrid teases him.

"What? It's true. We are known for our appearance."

I take that moment to study Aksel. His hair is so black it almost appears blue. It stops right at his shoulders and has subtle waves. His eyes are indigo-blue, and the chiseled edges of his jaw appear dangerously sharp. He does not have the muscular build of either Agnarr or Sten, but he is not small. He is just... lean. I recognize him but don't at the same time. The darkness behind his eyes remains the same.

"You do appear... different," I say.

"I am showing you more of my real self now that we don't have to hide anymore."

I'm going to need wine to survive this night. The hits just keep coming.

The gods must have heard my prayers. Agnarr pulls a jug of wine from his bag and guzzles some down. He will likely turn me down, but I don't care. I need to try. I want to drown my overwhelming thoughts.

I reposition myself beside him and hold my hand out. "May I?"

He remains silent, his eyes locked on the fire. I take his silence as a no and stand up to return to my original spot when he grabs my hand and pulls me back down. He hands me the jug, and I take a hefty sip. The liquid rushes down my throat and warms my body instantly.

"Thank you." I give him a soft small smile. He merely nods. Now I am ready, or at least partially ready, to ask Aksel, "What do you mean by real self?"

"We have the ability to alter our appearance, making it easier to blend in," Astrid answers for him.

"What do you usually look like?" Sten asks, clearly the most curious of us.

The twins shrug and transform right before our eyes. Aksel does not change much since he is already loosening the reins. The noticeable differences are that his hair reaches his mid-back, his skin darkens to a smoky quartz, and he has long earrings in both ears.

Astrid is... stunning. Her hair is so light it's almost white and reaches down to the curve of her arse. Her fair skin appears to shimmer in the light of the fire, and she has eyes that are the color of sapphires. The full pouty lips encasing her smile are the perfect shade of pink.

What really strikes me is how different they look from each other.

"Why are you so... opposite?" I ask.

"Good eye, Bryn." Astrid smiles. "I am a light elf, and Aksel is a dark elf."

"What is the difference?" Sten asks, no longer eating as he is fully vested in what is occurring.

"Customarily, light and dark elves are very different. We live in different worlds, but since Astrid and I were born from the same womb, we are unique. Astrid has constructive powers, while mine are more destructive," Aksel says.

"Like good and evil," I say.

Aksel nods. "That is a way to think of it. I have the ability of enchantment and to manipulate despair."

"And I have the ability to heal and manipulate time."

My mind immediately transports me back to when I almost killed myself in the forest. When I looked in the mirror, all my injuries were just gone. It was Astrid.

"You healed me. After my fall," I say, my eyes locking on Astrid's.

"Yes, I did."

I smile back, tears welling in my eyes. All this time I had someone looking out for me and I didn't even know it. I look over at Agnarr, but he is still lost in the fire. I'm not even sure he is listening.

"Alright, does anyone else have any wild secrets?" Sten asks. The silence is so thick it is painful. "You willing to share some of that wine with me, Agnarr?"

Agnarr looks right at him, chugs the rest of the bottle, and throws it into the fire before lying down on his fur.

Sten goes to say something else, and I shake my head. He begrudgingly nods in acceptance and lies back on his own fur. Astrid sits beside me and leans against me, just as she has always done. I lean back into her and close my eyes, thanking the gods for providing for me even when it didn't seem like it.

I RISE before the sun to enjoy the quiet of the forest. Mormor taught me the importance of finding stillness from an early age. How to not let myself be burned in the chaos and just utiseta. Utiseta, or sitting out, is an integral part of Viking tradition. It involves sitting outside with oneself to take an inner journey—an inward connection to seek wisdom and understanding. The gods know that after everything, I certainly need to reconnect with myself.

After wandering a short distance from our camp, I see a rock perfect for sitting out. I close my eyes and just disappear inside myself.

"I can't believe you still do this utiseta troll talk." Espen's voice echoes inside my head. He never did understand or like it. I enjoyed doing anything with Mormor.

"It's not troll talk, Espen, but you interrupting me is."

"And I was under the impression you missed me."

"Of course, I miss you. Why do you think I am using utiseta? I am trying to find wisdom and understanding. Right now, everything feels...in shambles."

"You will find the answers you seek, sis."

"Where and how?"

Just like that, he is gone. I squeeze the wooden pendant from his necklace to try to reconnect, but it doesn't work. Though I do so enjoy his...visits and our typical witty banter, it would be much more helpful if he actually told me something of value. I let out a deep sigh and try once again to find that inward connection.

By the time I make it back to camp, everyone is awake. Sten and Aksel appear to be looking at a map, Astrid is eating, and Agnarr... is still just sitting by the fire. Then it hits me. My map! I dash over to my bag and pull out the magic map I received from Telm.

Laying it out on a pile of debris, I watch as the map forms before my eyes, showing me what I asked to see the last time I made use of it. Sigvard. His dot still roams in the same area as before, in the safety of Fellheim. As I watch his dot move about the map, a new idea forms in my mind. A notion I would have never previously even considered.

"I know what we should do," I say, my eyes locked on the Sigvard dot.

"And what, pray tell, is that, Princess?" Aksel asks.

"We were planning to head toward Hitara," Sten says.

Hitara sits across Isvann Lake, far from the castle and Thornheim. It would require quite a journey.

"Ha!" Agnarr laughs, offering his first interaction since yesterday.

"What is so funn—"

"We are going to kidnap the king," I blurt out, interrupting Sten from starting another pissing contest with Agnarr.

"Someone please tell me I misheard her." Aksel looks around at the others.

"Even *if* we wanted to kidnap the king, that would not be an easy task, Brynja. There is a reason Sigvard hasn't done it," Sten says, trying to offer kind words yet still tell me why it's impossible.

"Or maybe Sigvard is just a coward," Agnarr says. He can't stop himself from doing anything to degrade Sten.

"I have many advantages Sigvard does not." I place my hands on either side of the map and look up at them. "I know the castle like the back of my hand, Orn is still there to offer assistance, and..."

I pause, unsure if I should say the last part. They are already questioning my sanity; if I continue, I may lose their faith entirely.

"And what?" Sten asks, forever the curious one.

"And I... we... have a dragon."

"Ahh, so you finally met Magnus!" Astrid says, smirking.

It is taking great effort for me not to be upset about all these secrets. I want to remain understanding that Astrid and Aksel did it to protect themselves and me, but each time a new secret arises, it leaves me wary.

"You know of Magnus?"

Astrid senses my uneasiness and moves beside me. "Yes. I know Magnus, and I knew Mormor Thorsson as well. Do you remember the small boy you quarreled with whenever you visited her?"

"Yes, of course," I say, confused where this is leading.

"That was me," Aksel says, smiling.

"I'm sorry… what?" I must have misheard him.

"We have been around your family for generations," Astrid says, composed, as if what she said wasn't a big deal. I, on the other hand, have lost my patience.

"Alright. I need to hear what secrets remain right this moment. I have handled all of this with grace and compassion, but I am losing my grip." I squeeze my hands tightly into fists. Astrid places a hand on my shoulder.

"We only kept these secrets to protect everyone involved an—"

"Protect everyone from what, exactly? While you were so-called protecting me, I was regularly beaten by my father. Held captive with nothing to eat. Told repeatedly that my worth was nothing. Oh! And my mother and brother were killed. So please tell me what you were so wonderfully protecting me from!" My anger and hurt no longer wish to be concealed.

"If our true identities had been revealed, your entire family would have been killed. Not all people of Midgard are as… understanding as your family," Astrid answers, her hand circling my shoulder. I want to throw it off.

"You were protecting yourselves. Not us."

"That is not true, Bryn."

"You can lie to yourself all you want, but not to me. Not anymore. What other secrets do you carry?" I push away from her.

"We have taken care of your family for the last eight hundred years and will continue to do so until our demise. I understand it doesn't seem or feel that way to you, but it is the truth," Aksel says. His voice has a level of compassion I have never heard from him before.

"Do not speak to me about truth." I glare at him before holding my arms out to the side in the shape of a Y. "Anyone else? Does anyone else have any secrets to share, or shall our focus return to the king?"

"Please don't be upset, Bryn. We love you," Astrid says. Her eyes are filled with sincerity.

"Good. Now. Let us plan on how we shall kidnap the king!" I decide to use my anger more constructively.

Everyone circles around me except Agnarr. As much as I want to leave him be, we need him. He knows the castle just as well, and he is an incredible warrior. I ask everyone to stay put and walk over to Agnarr.

"I know you hate me, and I don't blame you, but can you please put your feelings aside and help us? We will not be successful without you."

He sighs heavily but gives me the slightest smile. "I would not miss the opportunity to avenge Espen."

I offer him my hand, and he firmly grasps my forearm. When we return to the group, I look around at the people I have beside me. Despite our issues, we have come together to battle against evil. An evil that will finally have to answer for all the things he has done.

"It is time to get revenge for all the innocents the King

has slain." I say. "Soon, he will no longer be able to hide behind the castle walls."

ONCE WE DEVISE A PLAN, we begin the trek to the castle. I never imagined I would be returning there willingly. Many scenarios have played out in my head since leaving, including being dragged back and slowly tortured until my death. Instead, it is I who will do the dragging. I will leave the torture to Sigvard. As much as I want a pound of the king's flesh, I do not wish to place myself on his level. Even after everything, my mother would not want that either.

"Brynja, your turn. What's next?" Sten asks.

I had been totally lost in my own thoughts. I had not realized they were talking through the plan again step by step.

"Apologies, I was not listening."

A suggestion of annoyance hovers in his eyes. "We cannot falter if we want this plan to work. Everyone must know and be ready at every moment. Understood?"

"Yes, of course."

"Again!" The determined warrior in him blazes proudly as he basks in the ability to use his knowledge.

"What's his story?" Astrid whispers in my ear.

"I don't know much of it, but I do know that he sacrificed himself to save his family."

"Mm, and are you two..." She bumps her hip into mine.

"Astrid, are you serious? No! He is one of Sigvard's men and..." I stop myself because I am whisper-shouting.

"And what?" She raises an eyebrow and presses her lips together to stop herself from giggling.

"There is no interest." I glance over at Sten to ensure he isn't listening to us.

"From you or him?"

"Both. Now enough, or we will both be in trouble for not paying attention."

BY THE TIME we stop for the evening, I'm physically and mentally exhausted. Sten hounded us relentlessly, ensuring we memorized every movement. I could recite it all in finite detail in my sleep if required. What was truly surprising is that Agnarr did not argue or make any sort of curt remark the entire day.

I decide I want to rest near him, so I wait for him to make himself comfortable before putting my smaller fur next to him and lying down. I use my oversized fur to cover us both but still provide him space. He turns from his side to his back but doesn't protest my presence, which is enough for me. I close my eyes to drift off, but before doing so, I say my piece to Agnarr.

"I'm so sorry, Agnarr."

He does not say a word, and he does not need to.

I WAKE up what seems like mere moments later. I am so warm that a sheen of sweat has formed on my skin. Agnarr has me pulled into his arms. He is sound asleep, his head tucked into the crook of my neck. He looks utterly peaceful, and I don't have the heart to wake him, so instead, I curl myself up into his chest. He lets out a soft sigh and clutches me tighter. His familiar smell surrounds me, and I do what any intelligent woman would. I drift back off to sleep.

When dawn arrives, Agnarr is on the opposite side of the camp, and I wonder if the entire thing was just a dream. Did he just wait for me to fall asleep and move immediately so I wouldn't put up a fight? At least I was able to apologize. I know it will never fix or take away what was done, but that is all I am capable of doing.

I cannot worry about it now. With dawn here, sunrise will quickly follow, and we must begin our attack. One crucial thing I know about the king, he has never been an early riser.

The castle looks just as it did when I left, including the severed heads outside the palace walls left by Sigvard and his men. I never took note of who was coming and going from the camp while I was there, and now I wish I had. Perhaps we would have been able to intercept them and convince them to join us. We may be well prepared, but you can never have enough aid.

Astrid splits off from us, going toward the front of the castle while the rest of us head for the service entrance I so frequently used. Most of the servants will be awake, but they will also be off doing their morning duties: cooking, cleaning, and preparing the rooms for the day.

I gently open the door and peer my head in. No one is in sight. I quickly move inside and close the door, leaving the others while I check for any dawdlers.

It is quiet. So far, things are unfolding well.

I return to the door to let everyone in. Once inside, we pray to Freyr, to bring us good fortune and split off. I hold Espen's pendent in my palm and ask him to be by my side before moving into the next room.

I bolt through the servants' quarters, leading me to the castle's smallest library. This library holds books containing family history. Espen and I spent much time here as young children, learning about our family and heritage. On the far back wall, there is a hidden instrument that turns the wall 180 degrees into the adjoining room. The king had these built to confuse intruders if any were able to get inside.

I step into place and pull the contraption. It is loud, but if the plan is going well, no one should be around to hear it. On the opposite side, just as I had remembered, is the king's personal armory. Quickly, I step inside and turn the wall back into place.

The first thing I grab is his prized golden bow. It has been passed down for generations, but I have no memories of anyone using it. I begged and begged to use it, but the king told me I was not worthy of it. Mormor made me one, but it was never reliable. Always broke. Beside the bow is a large bag of arrows. I sling it over my back, followed by the bow.

I then grab as many weapons as possible and line them up against the wall near the door. Once I have moved everything that looks suitable for war, I say one final prayer and stride out the door.

Outside, the hallway is empty, but as I round the first corner, two guards are moving in my direction. Before they can utter a word, I let fly two arrows. One pierces a guard in the heart, while the other arrow goes straight through the second guard's eye. I stop momentarily at their bodies as their warm blood pools on the floor.

"I knew I was a good shot, just needed a proper bow." I am unable to stop the satisfied smile on my face.

I enter the next hallway and see another guard standing outside a room—the throne room, but why? He has not noticed my presence, so I quickly fire an arrow. It enters his ear, and before his body can crash to the floor, I dash over and catch him, guiding him down with my legs.

Across the hall from the throne room is another library. I drag his body inside before pressing my ear to the door of the throne room. This was not a part of the plan, but a guard outside the throne room is odd. If the king were inside, there would be at least three men on guard, not one.

"Where is the princess?" someone shouts.

"I don't know. It is not my duty to find her. It's yours!" a voice shouts back.

"You either tell us where she is, or we kill you instead."

That is all I need to hear. I burst through the doors and find Agnarr on his knees with three guards around him. Blood drips down his face, and my shock quickly yields to fury.

The arrows I release feel quick and slow collectively, like I am witnessing the scene unfold in slow motion. The first one penetrates straight through the middle of the guard's forehead, and he collapses into a heap. The second one isn't as accurate, hitting the guard in the crease of the shoulder just below his collarbone. The third is a gut shot, bringing the last guard to his knees. I have another arrow at the ready as I circle them. Agnarr merely stares, tongue-tied.

"Any last words?" I ask.

"Fuck you, you traitorous bitch," the guard with the shoulder injury spits at me.

"You are not my type, but perhaps Hel would be interested in your proposition." I fire my arrow into his heart.

The remaining guard goes to speak, but Agnarr slices off his head in one smooth movement. We lock eyes momentarily, but right now, there is no time for words. Together, we move through the rest of the palace until we find the others and a stack of bodies outside the king's bedroom door.

"What took you two so long? We were worried we would have to proceed without you," Aksel whispers.

"No need for that. We are here. Now, let's get what we came here for."

I push open the door. Just as expected, the king remains asleep and unaware of what is unfolding in his own castle. Agnarr, Sten, and Aksel stand at the foot of the bed as I climb on top of the king's chest and take a seat.

"What in the gods is hap—Brynja?"

"Hi Daddy," I say, making my voice sound cute.

"Where have you been? I was so worri—"

I pull my sword from the scabbard and hold the tip at the base of his throat. I wanted to toy with him longer, but I'm in no mood for his troll talk

"You truly think I am a muttonhead, don't you?" I ask, applying some pressure to the blade, but before he can answer, I continue. "The only thing you have ever worried about is power. I was merely a formality."

He laughs that evil, maniacal laugh he does when he thinks he has the upper hand. "You will never be able to kill me. You are too weak. Always have been, and you made Espen weak, too."

I swallow down the urge to stab him in the eye and jump off his chest. "You are right. I will never kill you, but Sigvard will, and I will enjoy watching every second."

His laugh turns into a cackle as he gets out of bed. "Which one of these stinkfarts is Sigvard?"

"None of them. We will offer you as a gift to Sigvard." I smile, putting my sword back in its scabbard.

"I would not put your sword away. Those three guards outside were only the beginning. You can try to take me, but you will never make it out that door alive," he says, pointing at the bedroom door.

The rumble of the king's guard echoes outside the door. We knew they would come. How many was the only unanswered question, but it doesn't matter. We have two things he could never prepare for.

Astrid and Magnus.

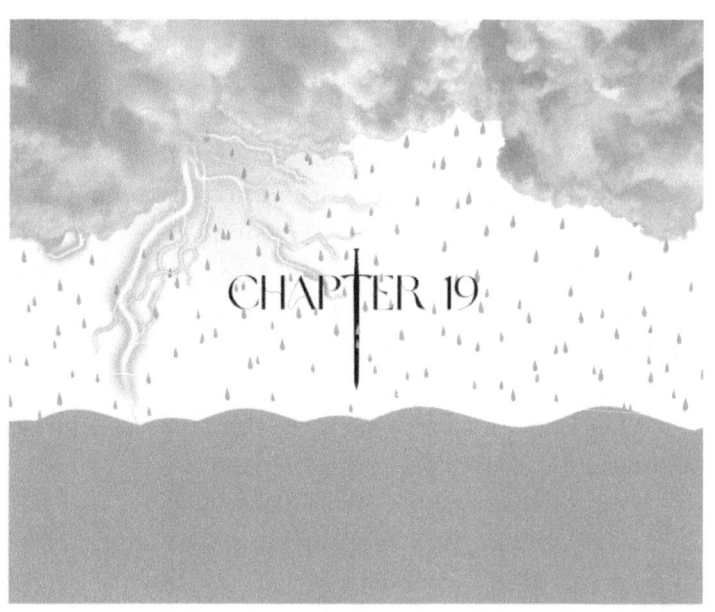

CHAPTER 19

The king reaches for a weapon hidden under his mattress, but Aksel gets to him first. His entire demeanor changes, like someone flipped a switch. He moves his mouth, but no words come out, and he appears... calm and unbothered. I have no time to process this newfound king as the door to the bedroom bursts open.

A sea of men floods into the room, and the true battle begins. My sword collides with one of the guards as Sten takes on the man beside me. It takes but a few slashes to fight them off, but another is quickly there to take their place. Several guards also try to reach the king, but they can't. He seems to be surrounded by some sort of invisible field.

Two men charge at me. Agnarr emerges and beheads one while I kneel and stick my blade through the second man's taint. He bellows out in pain as I remove my sword furiously, leaving him to bleed out.

The guards begin to work together and back us into the far corner. There is no secret door here, leaving us with no escape and very little room to defend. Three of them circle me, closing in tightly.

"Any last words, *Princess*?" one says, emphasizing the word with disgust.

I move so close to him that our noses touch. "You are not worthy of Valhalla."

When he goes to strike me, he freezes. Appearing just as a statue, he is stuck in place, unable to move.

"Way to cut it close," Sten laughs. As brave as I felt, there is no denying how hard my heart is pounding. I was fully prepared to meet Espen and my mother in the afterlife.

"Apologies. I got lost." Astrid walks through the bedroom door, speaking as if it is no big deal.

"Lost? How could you possibly get lost?" Sten asked, clearly annoyed.

"It doesn't matter. I am here, and we need to get out now. I can only hold them off for so long."

I bolt to the window and fling open the shutters. There is no sign of Magnus, and we are far too high to jump.

"You need to call her, Bryn," Astrid says.

"Call her? You mean just shout?"

"Normally your antics are adorable, but again I remind you, we don't have time."

"I'm not kidding, Astrid. I have no idea what you mean by 'call her.'"

"Use your mind. Just as you do when you talk to Espen."

How did she know about that? There is no time for questions, so I drop into my mind, hold Espen's pendant for good luck, and call to Magnus. I do it repeatedly, hoping that she will still hear me even if I only do it right once. I'm on the edge of losing hope when I see her.

Her wings span the entire horizon as she lets out a thunderous roar. Her purple scales shimmer brightly in the sunlight, and her chest glows deep red. As she gets closer, it dawns on me just how large she really is.

Agnarr shoves the king toward me. "Take this pile of rot with you."

Wait, they want me to jump out the window with the king? This is going to prove interesting. As Magnus draws closer, the guardsmen slowly begin to twitch.

"You really need to move faster," Astrid says.

"I can't do anything until Magnus is closer and you truly expect me just to leave all of you here? Absolutely not."

"Bryn, you don't have a choice. You either jump, or Aksel can push you."

I debate letting Aksel do it, as I feel he would have better aim, but I need to trust Magnus. She would not let me plummet to my death.

The guard closest to me blinks. Astrid's hold is weakening by the second. I am completely torn between not wanting to lose the king and abandoning my friends in the midst of battle.

The guard takes a step, and I suck in a breath, turning my attention back to the window. Magnus is closing the final bit of distance between us when the guard becomes completely unfrozen, his blade slicing toward me.

"Aksel, now!" Astrid shouts.

Instantly, I am thrown out the window with a force much stronger than I expected. The king catapults out with me and soars directly toward me.

I close my eyes and pray to the gods that we don't collide and fall to the earth. Air swirls around me, my hair entangling my face, and I feel like a rock being dropped into the ocean. I squeeze my eyes tighter, preparing for impact when I'm swept up into a warm body. A cascade of feathers spirals around me, blocking out everything, but it does stop my momentum.

"Hang on, Princess!" Magnus shouts as she dives through the sky. I have no clue what to grasp, but I hold tight the best I can manage. Her wings flap down, sending a gust of wind cascading as she turns away from the castle.

"No! Magnus go back!"

"I was instructed to get you out of here," she says.

"And I am telling you to go back. I will not leave them!"

Without another word, she turns back to the castle. The king is attempting to hang on to Magnus, but it's not easy with her smooth scales. The look on his face is absolute terror.

I push myself to stand and do my best to balance. Surprisingly, I feel more stable on my feet. Slowly, I move my position so I am centered on her back.

Standing firm, I pull out the golden bow and draw back an arrow. In rapid succession, I fire one after another into any guardsmen within my view, watching them fall like rocks in an avalanche. I attempt to fire several arrows into the window I jumped out of, but my timing is terrible, partially due to my fear of hitting my friends instead of the enemy. I can see they are getting overrun, and we need to get them out of there immediately.

"Magnus, can you handle four more?" I ask, reasonably certain of the answer.

"But of course, Princess, this was just not in the plan."

"Sometimes plans must be altered. Get us as close to the window as you can."

She swoops gracefully back toward the window as I watch, ready with an arrow, knowing full well we are putting ourselves at risk. The moment she is aligned with the window, I focus on the action inside. Quickly, I release several arrows, dropping more men to their knees.

"Agnarr! Quickly!" I yell. His head swivels around, and he shouts at the others.

Astrid and Agnarr run for us straight away. In a single bound, they are on Magnus's back, but I have yet to lay eyes on Aksel and Sten. Panic runs through me when I see Sten attempting to carry Aksel with one hand and fight off several guardsmen with the other. Only a few arrows remain, and I would risk hitting Sten, so I pull out my sword and jump back into the window.

I catch the first few men off guard, slicing them down with little effort, but once my presence is known, I am quickly the focus. My blade clangs against swords and axes coming from all directions, taking a heavy toll on my arms. It is one thing to hold off one sword, but an entirely different story when it is many.

A boot catches me in the back, knocking all the air out of my lungs and slamming me to the floor. I roll over onto my back just in time to avoid a sword to the heart. The guard raises his sword to make a final blow when a voice calls out.

"Guardsmen of the King, stop!" Everyone halts, and the room falls silent. "You should be ashamed of yourself. Attacking the princess as if she is the dishonorable one."

A hand is held out to me, and as I rise to my feet, I see who has bravely come to our rescue. Orn.

"She has dishonored not only the king but this entire realm," one of the men says.

"According to who? The king? Based on what knowledge? Please inform me." Orn raises one eyebrow as he pulls me into his side.

"She swore her loyalty to Sigvard. She is a traitor!" another man shouts.

Orn laughs bitterly. "You truly believe the princess would swear allegiance to a brute, and even if she did, can you blame her? Or have you all been blind to how the king has treated his entire family?"

This situation is not ideal, but I can't stop my heart from swelling with love. Not many times has someone come to my defense.

"You cannot stop us, Orn. Now begone before we kill you as well."

"You will have to kill me in order to get to Princess Brynja, so prepare yourselves for battle, mates."

I am flying through the air, pulled by Astrid's magic, before I can stop what is unfolding or even respond to Orn. I land square on my back on Magnus, with Aksel and Sten beside me. They are both bleeding, which sends a fiery rage through my veins. I attempt to go back to the window when Magnus soars away.

"No, Magnus, what are you doing? We can't leave Orn."

"Burn it! Burn it all to the ground!" I hear Orn shouting from the window as he shoves one of his once-trusted counterparts out the window to their deaths.

Magnus puffs up, the red in her chest now expanding throughout her body. In one giant exhale, a line of fire gusts out of her mouth and over the castle, spreading like ripples in a pool. I watch as the place I once called home erupts into a volcanic blaze, taking my past, including my sweet friend Orn. He who, without question, sacrificed everything for me so that I could move on and truly live.

This time, I have no quarrels with Magnus depositing us at Sigvard's camp. If he genuinely wishes to start a battle against a dragon twice the size of his entire camp, he deserves death.

Astrid uses her healing powers to tend to Aksel and Sten. I had not realized both possess the power to move objects, including people, telepathically. I had assumed only Aksel possessed the ability, but I was mistaken.

"Will you hold still, brute?" Astrid says, annoyed with Sten.

"No. Leave me be." He tries to inch away from her.

Clearly, this is not going well. I move over and sit beside Sten.

"Why will you not let Astrid help you?"

"I do not need help. It is just a few scratches. Each wound received in battle is a reminder of what not to do the next time." He gives me a very half-hearted smile.

"Oh? And what should you not do next time? Aid a friend who might otherwise be dead?"

"He is your friend, not mine. Which is a reminder, regardless of status, to not let emotions dictate what you do on the battlefield."

I wish I could argue with his logic, but I cannot, so I merely nod. I turn to Astrid and shake my head, letting her know she should just leave him be. He is no longer bleeding and does not appear in any sort of danger, so respecting his wish is the best course of action. She smiles shyly and nods.

When we arrive at Sigvard's camp, we are greeted by onlookers who keep their distance. I do not blame them, as Magnus could crush ten of them with one misstep of her claw. Once we have all dismounted from her great back, she winks and flies away. Agnarr and Astrid hold on to either side of the king as Sten leads the way to Sigvard. There is no telling how this will unfold, but I can't imagine it will be ill-received.

Just before we reach Sigvard's tent, Sten pauses and turns toward us.

"Let Brynja and me enter first. Once I call for you, you can bring in the king."

"Why shoul—"

"Agnarr, you have made your dislike for me clear, but I need you to trust me at this moment," Sten says, clearly biting back the desire to curse him.

Agnarr bites his lip but remains silent. With a nod of thanks, Sten and I enter Sigvard's tent.

He is sitting shirtless behind his usual table, waiting for us. I'm sure word of our return spread like wildfire.

"Look what Frigg dragged in. Or should I say dragon." He leans back in his chair, a smug look pulling across his lips.

"Apologies for my unexplained disappearance, but it was vital to the cause."

"You return to tell me why you are a traitor and expect me to listen? You are lucky you stand before me. You will now be removed, including every inch of your skin."

He snaps his fingers, and the two men inside the tent grab Sten.

"No! Stop! We have brought you a present. Perhaps you would like to see it first before wrongfully condemning your own man. You do not wish to be embarrassed, do you, Sigvard?" I ask, playing on his cocky emotions.

"There is nothing you could have possibly brought me that would change my mind," he laughs. The two men holding Sten follow suit.

"I wouldn't be so sure," I say, looking back at Sten, who smiles ever so slightly.

"Agnarr. Aksel. Please bring in Sigvard's present," Sten bellows.

"Delighted to see you brought additional company to my camp," Sigvard says, his voice layered with irritation and sarcasm.

Agnarr and Aksel enter the tent, dragging the king. Once Aksel's spell on him wore off, he has been as stubborn as an ox, resisting everything. He is well aware that once he is in Sigvard's possession, his life and his reign of blood are over.

Sigvard's eyes shift over the three of them, confused. It dawns on me that perhaps Sigvard does not recognize the king without his royal attire. Since we surprised him in the early hours, he only dons a pair of linen underwear.

"Sigvard, we are pleased to offer you this gift. The King of Midgard in his underwear," I say.

Sigvard's mouth falls open, first in utter disbelief and then in what appears to be skepticism.

"This cannot be the king." Sigvard points at the king, who is still trying to wiggle out of Aksel and Agnarr's grasps. "There is no way you four fools could have possibly done what my entire army could not." He turns away.

"That was never our mission, Sigvard, and you know it. We were trying to kill the king and his army. We never even considered kidnapping him as it was not an intelligent move. Brynja and Agnarr made that possible. They know the castle and the king's habits," Sten says, still held by Sigvard's men.

"I want you all out of my sight," Sigvard says, his back still facing us.

The king starts laughing, thinking he has caught a

break. I pray Sigvard is only in denial and will return to his wits soon.

"Sigvard, stop giving them Hel, that is the king. I would know his repulsive excuse for a being anywhere."

Thyra appears from behind the curtain that closes off the back of the tent. She appears to be wearing Sigvard's tunic. It is now my turn to be utterly shocked.

"Thyra?" I ask as if I don't recognize her.

"Hello, sweet friend. I'm happy to see you abandoned me for a just cause," she says, smiling. Her smile reflects both happiness and relief.

"I'm truly sorry for leaving you, but it appears it has worked out in everyone's favor." How long have I truly been gone? Did years pass, and I was unaware?

Sigvard moves closer to Thyra and places a hand on her stomach. "This man truly is the king?" He speaks only to her, like the rest of us are a figment of his imagination.

"Yes. I swear it. I worked under his unruly hand for many years. His face is one I would not forget," Thyra says, looking over his shoulder at me.

When Sigvard turns back to us, his demeanor has completely shifted. He grins at Sten and me before walking over to the king and grabbing his face forcefully.

"Welcome to the party, Your Majesty. This one is going to be a killer."

Chapter 20

- Sigvard

I cannot believe I am holding the king's face in my hand. I had been prepared to skin Sten alive for betraying the cause, but he shows up with the king and a handful of... misfits.

"You can release Sten and take this lovely treasure to the cage," I instruct.

My men immediately release Sten and drag the king off, kicking and cursing how this will be the death of me. As if he has any power here. It makes me laugh, and I look forward to our private chat later.

"Why don't you all get cleaned up and rest? We can celebrate this evening."

"How can we trust that you will not kill us in our

sleep?" the princess asks. I thought I was untrusting, but she gives me a run for it.

"I promise you are safe." I wave a hand in the air, not caring how they feel. This is my camp. If they do not feel safe, they can leave. I attempt to walk away and return to the peace of my private room when Thyra grabs my hand. Her skin is so soft it is like butter, and it swiftly brings me a sense of peace.

"Perhaps you should thank them. It might offer them more peace of mind," she says, smiling at me, her thumb rubbing over the rough edges of my hand.

The me who was once enslaved wants to argue with her and how it is not my job to placate them but the old me, the me that was not tainted by hate and despair, knows she is right. I will just not vocalize that part.

"Of course." I smile at her. I turn around to face Sten and his chaotic crew of deviants. "Thank you for delivering the king. You have proven you belong here."

With that, I disappear into my room, not wanting to be present for the peevish comments the princess will most certainly make. Thyra appears shortly after and sits on the bed, still warm from our fucking. I am ready to have her again, to feel her lustrous skin against mine. I sit beside her and kiss up her neck.

She nuzzles into me, and I cup her face with my palm.

"Sigvard, you need to be nicer to Brynja. She is not at all what you think her to be."

Every desire immediately drains from my body. I attempt to stand, but she places a hand on my thigh. "I will ask the same of her, but if I mean anything to you, you will do this for me."

Fuck. It has only been a short time, but I do not wish to disappoint Thyra. Even though everyone in camp has been enslaved, my connection and understanding with Thyra is unmatched.

"As long as you ask the same of her, I will do as you wish, but I have questions."

I have been wanting to ask Thyra why she is so dedicated to Brynja. She has sworn that she has always treated her as a friend, but how is that possible when she was forced to be a servant from a young age?

"Please. Ask away," she says, rubbing her hand on my thigh, reigniting my desire from before.

"Why do you care so deeply for Brynja?"

"She chose to befriend me regardless of the danger it put her in," she says, pausing briefly before continuing. "She never treated me like I was beneath her. Ever."

I may have misjudged the princess. The abuse she suffered at the hands of her own father cannot be ignored. Scars do not lie. I also trust Thyra. She has never given me a reason to doubt her, and if I am truly being fair, neither has the princess. We are more alike than I will ever be able to admit.

"I understand how important those types of friendships are. That is how Sten and I became friends," I say, giving her a peek into my bleak existence.

"You truly should treat him nicer instead of always questioning him." She smiles before kissing my cheek.

"Perhaps, but at this moment, that is the least of my worries."

My lips find hers. She kisses me tenderly, but it does not take long for her tongue to find mine. How this woman is able to be tender yet a sensual seductress at the same time will never make sense.

"Shouldn't we be preparing for tonight's festivities?" she asks, her lips still touching mine.

"We have plenty of time, and I have much more important work to tend to at this moment."

The time for talk is over. It is time I show this woman what kind of pleasures she has been missing out on. Having only experienced one man, she gives me the sensational opportunity to open up her world.

I slip my hands under the tunic, pulling her closer and allowing my hands to wander her bare skin. She purrs in my ear in response to my touch, causing goosebumps to form all over me. I pull her roughly onto my lap and yank the tunic off. Her hair falls in cascades around her back and shoulders.

I suck her nipple sharply into my mouth while one hand squeezes her ass and the other grips her neck. Watching my fingertips dig into her skin makes my dick swell. She had complete and utter trust I will not end her.

I switch to the other nipple before biting and kissing her all over. I attempt to continue my taste session when she gets out of my lap and drops to her knees between mine. Looping her thumbs into my waistband, she says one word. "Lift."

I lift my hips and let her slide my trousers off. I did not bother with any undergarments after our morning tryst, so there is nothing else left between us. Slowly and painfully, she begins kissing up my legs. Each kiss is softer than the next, leaving a trail of velvet warmth on my flesh. My cock is so engorged it is sending maddening waves of desire through every vein in my body.

I attempt to grip her hair and move her along, but she shakes her head, her lips gliding over me like feathers.

"You may get to push everyone else around, Sigvard, but not me," she says before licking my inner thigh.

"I cannot take much more of this torture," I grumble, impatient for her fulfillment.

"Then let me ease it some." She wraps her perfect pink lips around my cock and takes it to the hilt.

"Fuck, Thyra." I grab a handful of her hair.

She glides up slowly, using her tongue as a guide, causing my entire body to shudder. As slowly as she came up, she goes back down, and I can't decide if this is helping or making it worse. I squirm beneath her, and she grips my thighs tightly.

"You will sit here and enjoy," she says, nipping at my dick's head before wrapping her tongue around it and beginning the slow, tortuous journey down my shaft. My entire body floods with heat as waves of desire throb through me.

"I'm begging you, please let me feel you."

She stops and looks at me, her green eyes smoldering with satisfaction. "Is the great Sigvard begging me to spare him?"

"Yes. I am," I say, swallowing hard and praying to Freyja that this gorgeous creature will take pity on me.

She rises from her knees. A devious smile pulls at the corners of her lips. Without another word, she sits on my waiting cock, easing herself down. I wrap my hand around the back of her neck and force her to keep her eyes locked on me. The slow pace does not last long as our hunger overflows. Her supple ass is bouncing on my thighs, and I am prepared to throw her down on the bed when Henrik and Finn walk in.

I attempt to stop Thyra, but she merely glances over her shoulder and keeps going. Fuck, is she a temptress. Henrik and Finn stumble into each other multiple times before finally finding their way out of the tent.

I recapture her lips, more demanding this time before finding her earlobe.

"You are deliciously deviant," I say, biting her earlobe and throwing her down on the bed.

A hot tide of passion rages through me as I reenter her. She wraps her legs tightly around me as I hold her in place by the neck. Tears of arousal form in her eyes, and I release my grip, dropping myself on top of her, my lips kissing and biting the tender area of her neck divot.

She squeezes her thighs even tighter as her body instinctively arches to meet my thrusts. The pleasure moves from exquisite harmony to explosive as we climax. Her touch and our connection have officially torn my soul apart, and I'm not sure I can hide my pain any longer.

CHAPTER 21

I am lying on Sten's bed but cannot find sleep. I don't know what is plaguing me more: Orn sacrificing himself for us or Thyra and Sigvard. I feel like I missed several lifetimes while I was gone, but I am thankful that Thyra is not angry with me and for the influence she had on Sigvard. I knew turning over the king would come with mixed feelings, but I did not expect complete denial.

"You are supposed to be sleeping." Sten's voice travels over me.

"I know, but my mind is too busy keeping me awake." I rub my hands across my face.

"I wouldn't have sacrificed my bed if I had known it would only be used for thinking," Sten teases, lying beside me.

"Apologies. I will go walk around the camp instead."

I sit up to leave when Sten grabs my hand. "Don't go, I was merely being playful."

I collapse back on the bed, and it doesn't even shimmy due to Sten's size. I can't stop my mind from wondering how Agnarr would feel if he saw us lying here together.

"What is bothering you, Brynja?"

"Too many things. Orn. Thyra."

"I do have to admit, it was jarring to see Sigvard with Thyra."

"Has he not been with other women?" I ask, looking over at Sten.

"He has, but only for a night, and then he kicks them out." He clasps his hands behind his head.

"How about you?" The question falls from my lips before I can stop it, causing me to turn away from him.

"No. I am not fond of frivolous rendezvous," he says, rolling onto his side and leaning on his arm.

I laugh wholeheartedly as I expected a long list of conquests, not a no, followed by his dislike of one-night stands. I hope he does not ask me.

"You are full of pleasant surprises," I say, hoping to steer the conversation away from the cliff I sent it off.

"As are you."

He tucks a strand of my hair behind my ear. I am stunned by how much emotion I feel in such a simple gesture. I reach up and cup his face with my hand. His eyes close as I gently rub my thumb back and forth across his cheek.

When his eyes reopen, there is a flicker of longing that disappears just as swiftly as it appeared. Regardless, our eyes remain locked as we drift toward each other like the moon's pull. Our noses touch, bringing our lips so close I can feel the heat of his breath against my own.

"Sten! Are you here? It is time for wine and women," a voice calls out.

He is instantly on his feet to answer whoever barged in. I hear them exchange words and laughter before he peers back in at me.

"Are you ready to celebrate?" His joy has softened his features, making him appear younger.

"Of course." I smile back, bounding off the bed, wanting to share in his joy. This will be the first party I am able to attend without having to dress up and put on a show. I wonder whatever happened to Arik. He was a lovely man. I hope he escaped the king's wrath.

In the center of the camp is a bonfire so vast that Surtr, the fire giant, would be proud. Around it, everyone has gathered to drink and celebrate a freedom not felt through Midgard in ages. It was one thing to be a part of the rebellion but another to have the king held captive and his entire world destroyed. There will be no one coming for us tonight.

My eyes land on Thyra, perched on Sigvard's lap. She is smiling so heartily that her entire face glows. I have never seen her smile like that. I may not understand what she sees in Sigvard, but it must be something worthwhile for her to be so overjoyed.

"I guess we are even now, huh, Princess?"

I turn to see Agnarr. He is smirking and holding two mugs of wine. He walks the remaining distance between us and hands me the mug. I take a long drink, letting the wine warm me from teeth to toes.

"I supposed we can be even, but you never did accept my apology."

"At the time, I didn't, but when you dropped those guardsmen with your arrows... it changed."

"Oh, so all I had to do was save your life. I will

remember that for next time." I grin before taking another sip of wine.

"Where did you learn to shoot like that?" He takes a seat on a log near the fire. I sit directly beside him.

"I love the bow, but my father only let me use an inferior one. That gold one I stole from his armory. I begged him to let me use it, but he never would. It felt only fitting to use it on his own men. It is odd how... natural it felt. Like I had used it before."

"Perhaps you did, and you just don't recall?"

"I don't think so, Agnarr, but it's feasible.

"Princess! Ooooh Princess. I have good news!" Sigvard shouts from across the fire. I can't fathom what Sigvard views as good, and I am not in the mood for his antics, so I ignore his calls.

"Priiincess."

I roll my eyes and down the remnants of my wine. "Can I get you more wine?" I ask Agnarr, wanting any excuse to remove myself from his calls.

He nods but says, "You might just want to acknowledge him. I feel that ignoring him will only intensify his efforts."

I half smile at him and make it two steps before Sigvard calls out again.

"Do you not seek out a seer?"

This gets my attention. Thyra must have told him. I turn back, holding the empty cups at my side.

"I do. Why do you ask?"

"Because Wilde here is a seer." He points at a woman sitting nearby. She has long blonde hair that stops at her breasts. Numerous necklaces are hanging around her neck, and long pink feather earrings dangle from her ears. I hand the empty mugs to Agnarr and walk over to her. When I get close, I notice that one of her eyes is entirely white while the other is pink.

"You must be Brynja. Please sit with me."

She sits on the ground, legs crossed, with two other women behind her who are obviously twins. They look identical. I sit across from her, and she hands me a fresh mug. I bring it closer to my nose, and it is clearly not wine. It smells of rose and earth. I pause and look at her.

"Drink. It will help me connect with your inner being."

I do not know what she speaks about, but I do as requested. The drink doesn't taste good or bad, but it does send a searing pain through my chest. I clutch the front of my tunic as the air in my lungs seems to evacuate completely. Agnarr pulls me into his arms and tilts my head back.

"What have you done to her? She can't breathe!" The panic in his voice amplifies the fear already coursing through me. His fingers gently push my hair back as I watch his face fade in front of me.

"This is only temporary. She will be fine. Be patient."

"Be patient? She is turning blue!" Agnarr's voice sounds farther away with each word spoken.

The seer says something, but I have entirely faded into black.

I am falling. Falling so quickly that it feels like my entire reality is spinning. Air cyclones around me as lines of colors speed by. I feel as if I am lost somewhere between the heavens and life. Just as rapidly as it began, I slam into the ground, but there is no sense of pain. Finding my feet, I look around, but all that can be seen is the moving lines of color.

It reminds me of the stories of Heimdall and the Bifrost bridge. I have never seen the bridge with my own eyes, as only gods can cross it, but I imagine this is what it would look like. I walk closer to the moving colors and attempt to touch them, but my hand merely travels through, having no effect whatsoever.

Where am I, and what am I supposed to do here? Or have I willingly drunk a potion that sent me to the afterlife without a second thought?

I attempt to walk around my new location, but I am limited in how far I can travel. Instead, I lie back on the ground and watch the torrential sky above. The swirling colors begin to turn into familiar faces. First, Mormor appears. Then, Mother and Espen. They seem to be speaking to me, but I cannot hear their words. As they fade away, new faces appear, but they are not ones I recognize. Espen is trying to fight his way back through to me but is unsuccessful. It is as if he is in a lake, and his head keeps getting pushed back under the water's surface.

I reach up to him, knowing he is too far out of my reach, but wanting so badly to speak with him. Or even just touch him for but a moment. A spark flies from my finger and pulls Espen out of the murkiness, exposing more of his body. He reaches out for me, and I swear our fingers are only inches apart when the spark from my finger ignites, lighting the whole area like a lightning bolt.

I jolt upright, gulping in air as Agnarr pats my back.

"Holy fuck, she is alive," Sten says from somewhere around me.

My eyes are filled with tears, and I have to wipe them away in order to take in my surroundings.

Wilde remains in the same position but with runes scattered in front of her. She appears as dazed as I feel. Sten, Astrid, and Aksel have gathered around me, tears streaking their faces. It seems I am not the only one who thought I moved on to the afterlife. Astrid reaches out and grips my hand firmly.

"Princess, I am not sure how to tell you this, but the runes never lie," Wilde says.

"Whatever it is, it cannot be worse than what I just experienced." I struggle to find my breath.

"You are not who you think you are." Wilde touches each rune with her fingertips. Seers use runes to predict the future, cast spells, or even just to gain insight or knowledge.

"Not being a princess wouldn't be so bad." I try to make light of the fact that I almost perished. At least, I think.

Her eyes find mine. Even though the white eye has no center, I can tell she is looking at me deeply, attempting to prepare me for the words she is about to utter.

"You are not a princess. Every moment you have lived has not been your own."

"Okay, that is enough show and tell. C'mon Brynja." Agnarr helps me to my feet. I lean heavily on him as my legs feel like jelly. Sten comes to my aid as well, slinging my other arm around his neck. We begin to walk away when Wilde calls after us.

"You want the truth, do you not, Brynja?"

I tap both men on the shoulder to halt our progress and turn back to her.

"I do, but how do I know you speak the truth and it's not something Sigvard instructed you to say?"

"I do not serve Sigvard. I serve Odin."

A chill rushes down my spine so violently that my entire body shivers.

"Brynja, you need rest and warmth. Do not play into this witch's game," Agnarr says.

I shake my head. "No, I want to hear. Apologies for my disrespect, Wilde."

"None needed here. Please come sit and hold my hand, I will show you so there is no denying it." Sten sweeps me up into his arms and places me beside Wilde. She holds out her hand. "Brace yourself; this will be powerful but brief."

The moment our fingers clasp, a vision so clear flashes before me. I am riding a beautiful all white winged horse. My entire body is clad in white armor, and the white sword from my previous visions hangs from my hip. The golden bow that my father so cruelly kept from me is in my grasp, and I shoot golden arrows at a battle below. All around me are other alluring women riding winged horses with swords soaked in crimson, following my lead. Odin gives orders from above, lightning darting from his finger.

The world snaps back with brutal clarity as Wilde's fingers stroke my cheek.

She leans in, her voice dark with truth.

"You were never meant to wear a crown, my dear."

"You were made for war."

"You are a—"

"Valkyrie."

www.ingramcontent.com/pod-product-compliance
Lightning Source LLC
LaVergne TN
LVHW041757060526
838201LV00046B/1029